Merton snapped the elastic bands of the cabin seat around his waist and legs, then placed the electrodes of the sleep-inducer on his forehead. He set the timer for three hours, and relaxed. Very gently, hypnotically, the electronic pulses throbbed in the frontal lobes of his brain. Colored spirals of light expanded beneath his closed eyelids, widening outward to infinity.

The brazen clamor of the alarm dragged him back from his dreamless sleep. He was instantly awake, his eyes scanning the instrument panel. Only two hours had passed – but above the accelerometer, a red light was flashing. Thrust was falling; *Diana* was losing power.

Merton's first thought was that something had happened to the sail; perhaps the antispin devices had failed, and the rigging had become twisted. Swiftly, he checked the meters that showed the tension of the shroud lines. Strange – on the one side of the sail they were reading normally, but on the other the pull was dropping slowly, even as he watched.

In sudden understanding, Merton grabbed the periscope, switched to wide-angle vision, and started to scan the edge of the sail. Yes – th
was the trouble, and it could have only

A huge, sharp-edged shad
slide across the gle
Darkness was f
passed betwe
robbed of the
all thrust and d

Also by Arthur C. Clarke in paperback

THE DEEP RANGE

THE FOUNTAINS OF PARADISE

IMPERIAL EARTH

THE OTHER SIDE OF THE SKY

REACH FOR TOMORROW

TALES OF TEN WORLDS

ASTOUNDING DAYS

ARTHUR C CLARKE

THE WIND FROM THE SUN

VISTA

First published in Great Britain 1972
by Victor Gollancz Ltd

First VGSF edition published 1990

This Vista edition published 1996
Vista is an imprint of the Cassell Group
Wellington House, 125 Strand, London WC2R 0BB

A catalogue record for this book is
available from the British Library.

ISBN 0 575 60052 7

Printed and bound in Great Britain
by Cox & Wyman Ltd, Reading, Berks.

96 97 98 99 10 9 8 7 6 5 4 3 2 1

Affectionately dedicated to the
Hotel Chelsea,
friendly home of my late youth.

Preface

This volume contains all the stories I wrote in the decade of the '60's, which was one of the most dramatic periods in the entire history of science and technology. Those years embraced the laser, the genetic code, the first robot probes of Mars and Venus, the discovery of pulsars—and the landing on the Moon. Many of these events, either in anticipation or after achievement, are reflected in these tales; for that reason I have placed them in chronological order.

This is my sixth volume of short stories, and I was tempted to give it the subtitle "The Last of Clarke"—not through any intimations of mortality (I have every intention of seeing what *really* happens in the year 2001), but because I seem to be doing less and less writing, and more and more talking, traveling, filming, and skin-diving. Extrapolating from my present rate of production, volume seven would appear to lie so far in the future that it may be better just to add my occasional stories to later editions of this book.

"The Wind from the Sun" was called "Sunjammer" when it was first published, in *Boys' Life*. By one of those strange coincidences that often occur in literature (see "Herbert George Morley Roberts Wells, Esq."), Poul Anderson used the same title, almost simultaneously.

The concept of the lunar launcher in "Maelstrom II" was, I believe, first put forward in my paper "Electromagnetic Launching as a Major Contribution to Space Flight" (*Journal of the British Interplanetary Society,* November 1950).

The detailed predictions for the events that *will* take place as described in "Transit of Earth" were made by Jan Meeus (*Journal of the British Astronomical Association,* vol. 72, no.

6, 1962). I am greatly indebted to Mr. Meeus's paper for both information and inspiration.

The phrase "the Wheels of Poseidon" (in "A Meeting with Medusa") was coined by my friend the late Willy Ley, and the relevant quotations were taken from his book *On Earth and in the Sky*. The cause of this extraordinary and awe-inspiring phenomenon is by no means fully understood.

Finally, may I say that this volume can perhaps claim one modest record in "The Longest Science-Fiction Story Ever Told": no longer story ever has been written, or ever will be.

ARTHUR C. CLARKE

Colombo, Ceylon
February 1971

Contents

The Food of the Gods

It's only fair to warn you, Mr. Chairman, that much of my evidence will be highly nauseating; it involves aspects of human nature that are very seldom discussed in public, and certainly not before a congressional committee. But I am afraid that they have to be faced; there are times when the veil of hypocrisy has to be ripped away, and this is one of them.

You and I, gentlemen, have descended from a long line of carnivores. I see from your expressions that most of you don't recognize the term. Well, that's not surprising—it comes from a language that has been obsolete for two thousand years. Perhaps I had better avoid euphemisms and be brutally frank, even if I have to use words that are never heard in polite society. I apologize in advance to anyone I may offend.

Until a few centuries ago, the favorite food of almost all men was *meat*—the *flesh* of once living animals. I'm not trying to turn your stomachs; this is a simple statement of fact, which you can check in any history book. . . .

Why, certainly, Mr. Chairman. I'm quite prepared to wait until Senator Irving feels better. We professionals sometimes forget how laymen may react to statements like that. At the same time, I must warn the committee that there is very much worse to come. If any of you gentlemen are at all squeamish, I suggest you follow the Senator before it's too late. . . .

Well, if I may continue. Until modern times, all food fell into two categories. Most of it was produced from plants—cereals, fruits, plankton, algae, and other forms of vegetation. It's hard for us to realize that the vast majority of our ancestors were farmers, winning food from land or sea by primitive and often backbreaking techniques; but that is the truth.

The second type of food, if I may return to this unpleasant subject, was meat, produced from a relatively small number of animals. You may be familiar with some of them—cows, pigs, sheep, whales. Most people—I am sorry to stress this, but the fact is beyond dispute—preferred meat to any other food, though only the wealthiest were able to indulge this appetite. To most of mankind, meat was a rare and occasional delicacy in a diet that was more than ninety-per-cent vegetable.

If we look at the matter calmly and dispassionately—as I hope Senator Irving is now in a position to do—we can see that meat was bound to be rare and expensive, for its production is an extremely inefficient process. To make a kilo of meat, the animal concerned had to eat at least ten kilos of vegetable food—very often food that could have been consumed directly by human beings. Quite apart from any consideration of aesthetics, this state of affairs could not be tolerated after the population explosion of the twentieth century. Every man who ate meat was condemning ten or more of his fellow humans to starvation. . . .

Luckily for all of us, the biochemists solved the problem; as you may know, the answer was one of the countless by-products of space research. All food—animal or vegetable—is built up from a very few common elements. Carbon, hydrogen, oxygen, nitrogen, traces of sulphur and phosphorus—these half-dozen elements, and a few others, combine in an almost infinite variety of ways to make up every food that man has ever eaten or ever will eat. Faced with the problem of colonizing the Moon and planets, the biochemists of the twenty-first century discovered how to synthesize any desired food from the basic raw materials of water, air, and rock. It was the greatest, and perhaps the most important, achievement in the history of science. But we should not feel too proud of it. The vegetable kingdom had beaten us by a billion years.

The chemists could now synthesize any conceivable food, whether it had a counterpart in nature or not. Needless to say, there were mistakes—even disasters. Industrial empires rose and crashed; the switch from agriculture and animal husbandry to the giant automatic processing plants and omniverters of today was often a painful one. But it had to be made, and we are the better for it. The danger of starvation has been banished forever, and we have a richness and variety of food that no other age has ever known.

In addition, of course, there was a moral gain. We no longer murder millions of living creatures, and such revolting institutions as the slaughterhouse and the butcher shop have vanished from the face of the Earth. It seems incredible to us that even our ancestors, coarse and brutal though they were, could ever have tolerated such obscenities.

And yet—it is impossible to make a clean break with the past. As I have already remarked, we are carnivores; we inherit tastes and appetites that have been acquired over a million years of time. Whether we like it or not, only a few years ago some of our great-grandparents were enjoying the flesh of cattle and sheep and pigs—when they could get it. *And we still enjoy it today. . . .*

Oh dear, maybe Senator Irving had better stay outside from now on. Perhaps I should not have been quite so blunt. What I meant, of course, was that many of the synthetic foods we now eat have the same formula as the old natural products; some of them, indeed, are such exact replicas that no chemical or other test could reveal any difference. This situation is logical and inevitable; we manufacturers simply took the most popular presynthetic foods as our models, and reproduced their taste and texture.

Of course, we also created new names that didn't hint of an anatomical or zoological origin, so that no one would be reminded of the facts of life. When you go into a restaurant, most of the words you'll find on the menu have been invented since the beginning of the twenty-first century, or else adapted from French originals that few people would recognize. If you ever want to find your threshold of tolerance, you can try an interesting but highly unpleasant experiment. The classified section of the Library of Congress has a large number of menus from famous restaurants—yes, and White House banquets—going back for five hundred years. They have a crude, dissecting-room frankness that makes them almost unreadable. I cannot think of anything that reveals more vividly the gulf between us and our ancestors of only a few generations ago. . . .

Yes, Mr. Chairman—I *am* coming to the point; all this is highly relevant, however disagreeable it may be. I am not trying to spoil your appetites; I am merely laying the groundwork for the charge I wish to bring against my competitor, Triplanetary Food Corporation. Unless you understand this background, you may think that this is a frivolous complaint inspired by the admittedly serious losses my firm has sustained since Ambrosia Plus came on the market.

New foods, gentlemen, are invented every week. It is hard to keep track of them. They come and go like women's fashions, and only one in a thousand becomes a permanent addition to the menu. It is *extremely* rare for one to hit the public fancy overnight, and I freely admit that the Ambrosia Plus line of dishes has been the greatest success in the entire history of food manufacture. You all know the position: everything else has been swept off the market.

Naturally, we were forced to accept the challenge. The biochemists of my organization are as good as any in the solar system, and they promptly got to work on Ambrosia Plus. I am not giving away any trade secrets when I tell you that we have tapes of practically every food, natural or synthetic, that has ever been eaten by mankind—right back to exotic items that you've never heard of, like fried squid, locusts in honey, peacocks' tongues, Venusian polypod. . . . Our enormous library of flavors and textures is our basic stock in trade, as it is with all firms in the business. From it we can select and mix items in any conceivable combination; and usually we can duplicate, without too much trouble, any product that our competitors put out.

But Ambrosia Plus had us baffled for quite some time. Its protein-fat breakdown classified it as a straightforward meat, without too many complications—yet we couldn't match it exactly. It was the first time my chemists had failed; not one of them could explain just what gave the stuff its extraordinary appeal—which, as we all know, makes every other food seem insipid by comparison. As well it might . . . but I am getting ahead of myself.

Very shortly, Mr. Chairman, the president of Triplanetary Foods will be appearing before you—rather reluctantly, I'm sure. He will tell you that Ambrosia Plus is synthesized from air, water, limestone, sulphur, phosphorus, and the rest. That will be perfectly true, but it will be the least important part of the story. For we have now discovered his secret—which, like most secrets, is very simple once you know it.

I really must congratulate my competitor. He has at last made available unlimited quantities of what is, from the nature of things, the ideal food for mankind. Until now, it has been in extremely short supply, and therefore all the more relished by the few connoisseurs who could obtain it. Without exception, they have sworn that nothing else can remotely compare with it.

Yes, Triplanetary's chemists have done a superb technical job. Now *you* have to resolve the moral and philosophical issues. When I began my evidence, I used the archaic word "carnivore." Now I must introduce you to another: I'll spell it out the first time: C-A-N-N-I-B-A-L. . . .

May 1961

Maelstrom II

He was not the first man, Cliff Leyland told himself bitterly, to know the exact second and the precise manner of his death. Times beyond number, condemned criminals had waited for their last dawn. Yet until the very end they could hope for a reprieve; human judges can show mercy. But against the laws of nature, there is no appeal.

And only six hours ago, he had been whistling happily while he packed his ten kilos of personal baggage for the long fall home. He could still remember (even now, after all that had happened) how he had dreamed that Myra was already in his arms, that he was taking Brian and Sue on that promised cruise down the Nile. In a few minutes, as Earth rose above the horizon, he might see the Nile again; but memory alone could bring back the faces of his wife and children. And all because he had tried to save nine hundred and fifty sterling dollars by riding home on the freight catapult, instead of the rocket shuttle.

He had expected the first twelve seconds of the trip to be rough, as the electric launcher whipped the capsule along its ten-mile track and shot him off the Moon. Even with the protection of the water-bath in which he would float during countdown, he had not looked forward to the twenty g's of take-off. Yet when the acceleration had gripped the capsule, he had been hardly aware of the immense forces acting upon him. The only sound was a faint creaking from the metal walls; to anyone who had experienced the thunder of a rocket launch, the silence was uncanny. When the cabin speaker had announced "T plus five seconds; speed two thousand miles an hour," he could scarcely believe it.

Two thousand miles an hour in five seconds from a standing start—with seven seconds still to go as the generators smashed their thunderbolts of power into the launcher. He was riding the lightning across the face of the Moon. And at T plus seven seconds, the lightning failed.

Even in the womblike shelter of the tank, Cliff could sense that something had gone wrong. The water around him, until now frozen almost rigid by its weight, seemed suddenly to become alive. Though the capsule was still hurtling along the track, all acceleration had ceased, and it was merely coasting under its own momentum.

He had no time to feel fear, or to wonder what had happened, for the power failure lasted little more than a second. Then, with a jolt that shook the capsule from end to end and set off a series of ominous, tinkling crashes, the field came on again.

When the acceleration faded for the last time, all weight vanished with it. Cliff needed no instrument but his stomach to tell that the capsule had left the end of the track and was rising away from the surface of the Moon. He waited impatiently until the automatic pumps had drained the tank and the hot-air driers had done their work; then he drifted across the control panel, and pulled himself down into the bucket seat.

"Launch Control," he called urgently, as he drew the restraining straps around his waist, "what the devil happened?"

A brisk but worried voice answered at once.

"We're still checking—call you back in thirty seconds." Then it added belatedly, "Glad you're O.K."

While he was waiting, Cliff switched to forward vision. There was nothing ahead except stars—which was as it should be. At least he had taken off with most of his planned speed, and there was no danger that he would crash back to the Moon's surface immediately. But he would crash back sooner or later, for he could not possibly have reached escape velocity. He must be rising out into space along a great ellipse—and, in a few hours, he would be back at his starting point.

"Hello, Cliff," said Launch Control suddenly. "We've found what happened. The circuit breakers tripped when you went through section five of the track. So your take-off speed was seven hundred miles an hour low. That will bring you back in just over five hours—but don't worry; your course-correction jets can boost you into a stable orbit. We'll tell you when to fire them. Then all you have to do is to sit tight until we can send someone to haul you down."

Slowly, Cliff allowed himself to relax. He had forgotten the capsule's vernier rockets. Low-powered though they were, they could kick him into an orbit that would clear the Moon. Though he might fall back to within a few miles of the lunar surface, skimming over mountains and plains at a breath-taking speed, he would be perfectly safe.

Then he remembered those tinkling crashes from the control compartment, and his hopes dimmed again, for there were not many things that could break in a space vehicle without most unpleasant consequences.

He was facing those consequences, now that the final checks of the ignition circuits had been completed. Neither on MANUAL nor on AUTO would the navigation rockets fire. The capsule's modest fuel reserves, which could have taken him to safety, were utterly useless. In five hours he would complete his orbit—and return to his launching point.

I wonder if they'll name the new crater after me, thought Cliff. "Crater Leyland: diameter . . ." What diameter? Better not exaggerate—I don't suppose it will be more than a couple of hundred yards across. Hardly worth putting on the map.

Launch Control was still silent, but that was not surprising. There was little that one could say to a man already as good as dead. And yet, though he knew that nothing could alter his trajectory, even now he could not believe that he would soon be scattered over most of Farside. He was still soaring away from the Moon, snug and comfortable in his little cabin. The idea of death was utterly incongruous—as it is to all men until the final second.

And then, for a moment, Cliff forgot his own problem.

The horizon ahead was no longer flat. Something more brilliant even than the blazing lunar landscape was lifting against the stars. As the capsule curved round the edge of the Moon, it was creating the only kind of earthrise that was possible—a man-made one. In a minute it was all over, such was his speed in orbit. By that time the Earth had leaped clear of the horizon, and was climbing swiftly up the sky.

It was three-quarters full, and almost too bright to look upon. Here was a cosmic mirror made not of dull rocks and dusty plains, but of snow and cloud and sea. Indeed, it was almost all sea, for the Pacific was turned toward him, and the blinding reflection of the sun covered the Hawaiian Islands. The haze of the atmosphere—that soft blanket that should have cushioned his descent in a few hours' time—obliterated all geographical details; perhaps that darker patch emerging from night was New Guinea, but he could not be sure.

There was a bitter irony in the knowledge that he was heading straight toward that lovely, gleaming apparition. Another seven hundred miles an hour and he would have made it. Seven hundred miles an hour—that was all. He might as well ask for seven million.

The sight of the rising Earth brought home to him, with irresistible force, the duty he feared but could postpone no longer.

"Launch Control," he said, holding his voice steady with a great effort, "please give me a circuit to Earth."

This was one of the strangest things he had ever done in his life: to sit here above the Moon and listen to the telephone ring in his own home, a quarter of a million miles away. It must be near midnight down there in Africa, and it would be some time before there would be any answer. Myra would stir sleepily; then, because she was a spaceman's wife, always alert for disaster, she would be instantly awake. But they had both hated to have a phone in the bedroom, and it would be at least fifteen seconds before she could switch on the light, close the nursery door to avoid disturbing the baby, get down the stairs, and . . .

Her voice came clear and sweet across the emptiness of space. He would recognize it anywhere in the universe, and he detected at once the undertone of anxiety.

"Mrs. Leyland?" said the Earthside operator. "I have a call from your husband. Please remember the two-second time lag."

Cliff wondered how many people were listening to this call, on either the Moon, the Earth, or the relay satellites. It was hard to talk for the last time to your loved ones when you didn't know how many eavesdroppers there might be. But as soon as he began to speak, no one else existed but Myra and himself.

"Darling," he began, "this is Cliff. I'm afraid I won't be coming home, as I promised. There's been a . . . a technical slip. I'm quite all right at the moment, but I'm in big trouble."

He swallowed, trying to overcome the dryness in his mouth, then went on quickly before she could interrupt. As briefly as he could, he explained the situation. For his own sake as well as hers, he did not abandon all hope.

"Everyone's doing their best," he said. "Maybe they can get a ship up to me in time. But in case they can't . . . well, I wanted to speak to you and the children."

She took it well, as he had known that she would. He felt pride as well as love when her answer came back from the dark side of Earth.

"Don't worry, Cliff. I'm sure they'll get you out, and we'll have our holiday after all, exactly the way we planned."

"I think so, too," he lied. "But just in case, would you wake the children? Don't tell them that anything's wrong."

It was an endless half-minute before he heard their sleepy, yet excited, voices. Cliff would willingly have given these last few hours of his life to have seen their faces once again, but the capsule was not equipped with such luxuries as vision. Perhaps it was just as well, for he could not have hidden the truth had he looked into their eyes. They would know it soon enough, but not from him. He wanted to give them only happiness in these last moments together.

Yet it was hard to answer their questions, to tell them that he would soon be seeing them, to make promises that he could not keep. It needed all his self control when Brian reminded him of the moondust he had forgotten once before—but had remembered this time.

"I've got it, Brian; it's in a jar right beside me. Soon you'll be able to show it to your friends." (No: soon it will be back on the world from which it came.) "And Susie—be a good girl and do everything that Mummy tells you. Your last school report wasn't too good, you know, especially those remarks about behavior. . . . Yes, Brian, I have those photographs, and the piece of rock from Aristarchus. . . ."

It was hard to die at thirty-five; but it was hard, too, for a boy to lose his father at ten. How would Brian remember him in the years ahead? Perhaps as no more than a fading voice from space, for he had spent so little time on Earth. In the last few minutes, as he swung outward and then back to the Moon, there was little enough that he could do except project his love and his hopes across the emptiness that he would never span again. The rest was up to Myra.

When the children had gone, happy but puzzled, there was work to do. Now was the time to keep one's head, to be businesslike and practical. Myra must face the future without him, but at least he could make the transition easier. Whatever happens to the individual, life goes on; and to modern man life involves mortgages and installments due, insurance policies and joint bank accounts. Almost impersonally, as if they concerned someone else—which would soon be true enough—Cliff began to talk about these things. There was a time for the heart and a time for the brain. The heart would have its final say three hours from now, when he began his last approach to the surface of the Moon.

No one interrupted them. There must have been silent monitors maintaining the link between two worlds, but the two of them might have been the only people alive. Sometimes while he was speaking Cliff's eyes would stray to the periscope, and be dazzled by the glare of Earth—now more than halfway up the sky. It was impossible to believe that it was home for seven billion souls. Only three mattered to him now.

It should have been four, but with the best will in the world he could not put the baby on the same footing as the others. He had never seen his younger son; and now he never would.

At last he could think of no more to say. For some things, a lifetime was not enough—but an hour could be too much. He felt physically and emotionally exhausted, and the strain on Myra must have been equally great. He wanted to be alone with his thoughts and with the stars, to compose his mind and to make his peace with the universe.

"I'd like to sign off for an hour or so, darling," he said. There was no need for explanations; they understood each other too well. "I'll call you back in—in plenty of time. Good-by for now."

He waited the two and a half seconds for the answering good-by from Earth; then he cut the circuit and stared blankly at the tiny control desk. Quite unexpectedly, without desire or volition, tears sprang from his eyes, and suddenly he was weeping like a child.

He wept for his family, and for himself. He wept for the future that might have been, and the hopes that would soon be incandescent vapor, drifting between the stars. And he wept because there was nothing else to do.

After a while he felt much better. Indeed, he realized that he was extremely hungry. There was no point in dying on an empty stomach, and he began to rummage among the space rations in the closet-sized galley. While he was squeezing a tube of chicken-and-ham paste into his mouth, Launch Control called.

There was a new voice at the end of the line—a slow, steady, and immensely competent voice that sounded as if it would brook no nonsense from inanimate machinery.

"This is Van Kessel, Chief of Maintenance, Space Vehicles Division. Listen carefully, Leyland. We think we've found a way out. It's a long shot—but it's the only chance you have."

Alternations of hope and despair are hard on the nervous system. Cliff felt a sudden dizziness; he might have fallen had there been any direction in which to fall.

"Go ahead," he said faintly, when he had recovered. Then he listened to Van Kessel with an eagerness that slowly changed to incredulity.

"I don't believe it!" he said at last. "It just doesn't make sense!"

"You can't argue with the computers," answered Van Kessel. "They've checked the figures about twenty different ways. And it makes sense, all right. You won't be moving so fast at apogee, and it doesn't need much of a kick then to change your orbit. I suppose you've never been in a deep-space rig before?"

"No, of course not."

"Pity—but never mind. If you follow instructions, you can't go wrong. You'll find the suit in the locker at the end of the cabin. Break the seals and haul it out."

Cliff floated the full six feet from the control desk to the rear of the cabin and pulled on the lever marked EMERGENCY ONLY—TYPE 17 DEEP-SPACE SUIT. The door opened, and the shining silver fabric hung flaccid before him.

"Strip down to your underclothes and wriggle into it," said Van Kessel. "Don't bother about the biopack—you clamp that on later."

"I'm in," said Cliff presently. "What do I do now?"

"You wait twenty minutes—and then we'll give you the signal to open the air lock and jump."

The implications of that word "jump" suddenly penetrated. Cliff looked around the now familiar, comforting little cabin, and then thought of the lonely emptiness between the stars—the unreverberant abyss through which a man could fall until the end of time.

He had never been in free space; there was no reason why he should. He was just a farmer's boy with a master's degree in agronomy, seconded from the Sahara Reclamation Project and trying to grow crops on the Moon. Space was not for him;

he belonged to the worlds of soil and rock, of moondust and vacuum-formed pumice.

"I can't do it," he whispered. "Isn't there any other way?"

"There's not," snapped Van Kessel. "We're doing our damnedest to save you, and this is no time to get neurotic. Dozens of men have been in far worse situations—badly injured, trapped in wreckage a million miles from help. But you're not even scratched, and already you're squealing! Pull yourself together—or we'll sign off and leave you to stew in your own juice."

Cliff turned slowly red, and it was several seconds before he answered.

"I'm all right," he said at last. "Let's go through those instructions again."

"That's better," said Van Kessel approvingly. "Twenty minutes from now, when you're at apogee, you'll go into the air lock. From that point, we'll lose communication; your suit radio has only a ten-mile range. But we'll be tracking you on radar and we'll be able to speak to you when you pass over us again. Now, about the controls on your suit . . ."

The twenty minutes went quickly enough. At the end of that time, Cliff knew exactly what he had to do. He had even come to believe that it might work.

"Time to bail out," said Van Kessel. "The capsule's correctly oriented—the air lock points the way you want to go. But direction isn't critical. *Speed* is what matters. Put everything you've got into that jump—and good luck!"

"Thanks," said Cliff inadequately. "Sorry that I . . ."

"Forget it," interrupted Van Kessel. "Now get moving!"

For the last time, Cliff looked around the tiny cabin, wondering if there was anything that he had forgotten. All his personal belongings would have to be abandoned, but they could be replaced easily enough. Then he remembered the little jar of moondust he had promised Brian; this time, he would not let the boy down. The minute mass of the sample—only a few ounces—would make no difference to his fate. He tied a piece of string around the neck of the jar and attached it to the harness of his suit.

The air lock was so small that there was literally no room to move; he stood sandwiched between inner and outer doors until the automatic pumping sequence was finished. Then the wall slowly opened away from him, and he was facing the stars.

With his clumsy gloved fingers, he hauled himself out of the air lock and stood upright on the steeply curving hull, bracing himself tightly against it with the safety line. The splendor of the scene held him almost paralyzed. He forgot all his fears of vertigo and insecurity as he gazed around him, no longer constrained by the narrow field of vision of the periscope.

The Moon was a gigantic crescent, the dividing line between night and day a jagged arch sweeping across a quarter of the sky. Down there the sun was setting, at the beginning of the long lunar night, but the summits of isolated peaks were still blazing with the last light of day, defying the darkness that had already encircled them.

That darkness was not complete. Though the sun had gone from the land below, the almost full Earth flooded it with glory. Cliff could see, faint but clear in the glimmering earthlight, the outlines of seas and highlands, the dim stars of mountain peaks, the dark circles of craters. He was flying above a ghostly, sleeping land—a land that was trying to drag him to his death. For now he was poised at the highest point of his orbit, exactly on the line between Moon and Earth. It was time to go.

He bent his legs, crouching against the hull. Then, with all his force, he launched himself toward the stars, letting the safety line run out behind him.

The capsule receded with surprising speed, and as it did so, he felt a most unexpected sensation. He had anticipated terror or vertigo, but not this unmistakable, haunting sense of familiarity. All this had happened before; not to him, of course, but to someone else. He could not pinpoint the memory, and there was no time to hunt for it now.

He flashed a quick glance at Earth, Moon, and receding spacecraft, and made his decision without conscious thought.

The line whipped away as he snapped the quick-release. Now he was alone, two thousand miles above the Moon, a quarter of a million miles from Earth. He could do nothing but wait; it would be two and a half hours before he would know if he could live—and if his own muscles had performed the task that the rockets had failed to do.

And as the stars slowly revolved around him, he suddenly knew the origin of that haunting memory. It was many years since he had read Poe's short stories, but who could ever forget them?

He, too, was trapped in a maelstrom, being whirled down to his doom; he, too, hoped to escape by abandoning his vessel. Though the forces involved were totally different, the parallel was striking. Poe's fisherman had lashed himself to a barrel because stubby, cylindrical objects were being sucked down into the great whirlpool more slowly than his ship. It was a brilliant application of the laws of hydrodynamics. Cliff could only hope that his use of celestial mechanics would be equally inspired.

How fast had he jumped away from the capsule? At a good five miles an hour, surely. Trivial though that speed was by astronomical standards, it should be enough to inject him into a new orbit—one that, Van Kessel had promised him, would clear the Moon by several miles. That was not much of a margin, but it would be enough on this airless world, where there was no atmosphere to claw him down.

With a sudden spasm of guilt, Cliff realized that he had never made that second call to Myra. It was Van Kessel's fault; the engineer had kept him on the move, given him no time to brood over his own affairs. And Van Kessel was right: in a situation like this, a man could think only of himself. All his resources, mental and physical, must be concentrated on survival. This was no time or place for the distracting and weakening ties of love.

He was racing now toward the night side of the Moon, and the daylit crescent was shrinking as he watched. The intolerable disc of the Sun, at which he dared not look, was falling swiftly toward the curved horizon. The crescent moonscape dwindled to a burning line of light, a bow of fire set against the stars. Then the bow fragmented into a dozen shining beads, which one by one winked out as he shot into the shadow of the Moon.

With the going of the Sun, the earthlight seemed more brilliant than ever, frosting his suit with silver as he rotated slowly along his orbit. It took him about ten seconds to make each revolution; there was nothing he could do to check his spin, and indeed he welcomed the constantly changing view. Now that his eyes were no longer distracted by occasional glimpses of the Sun, he could see the stars in thousands, where there had been only hundreds before. The familiar constellations were drowned, and even the brightest of the planets were hard to find in that blaze of light.

The dark disc of the lunar night land lay across the star field like an eclipsing shadow, and it was slowly growing as he fell toward it. At every instant some star, bright or faint, would pass behind its edge and wink out of existence. It was almost as if a hole were growing in space, eating up the heavens.

There was no other indication of his movement, or of the passage of time—except for his regular ten-second spin. When he looked at his watch, he was astonished to see that he had left the capsule half an hour ago. He searched for it among the stars, without success. By now, it would be several miles behind. But presently it would draw ahead of him, as it moved on its lower orbit, and would be the first to reach the Moon.

Cliff was still puzzling over this paradox when the strain of the last few hours, combined with the euphoria of weightlessness, produced a result he would hardly have believed possible. Lulled by the gentle susurration of the air inlets, floating lighter than any feather as he turned beneath the stars, he fell into a dreamless sleep.

When he awoke at some prompting of his subconscious, the Earth was nearing the edge of the Moon. The sight almost brought on another wave of self-pity, and for a moment he had to fight for control of his emotions. This was the very last he might ever see of Earth, as his orbit took him back over Farside, into the land where the earthlight never shone. The brilliant antarctic icecaps, the equatorial cloud belts, the scintillation of the Sun upon the Pacific—all were sinking swiftly behind the lunar mountains. Then they were gone; he had neither Sun nor Earth to light him now, and the invisible land below was so black that it hurt his eyes.

Unbelievably, a cluster of stars had appeared *inside* the darkened disc, where no stars could possibly be. Cliff stared at them in astonishment for a few seconds, then realized he was passing above one of the Farside settlements. Down there beneath the pressure domes of their city, men were waiting out the lunar night—sleeping, working, loving, resting, quarreling. Did they know that he was speeding like an invisible meteor through their sky, racing above their heads at four thousand miles an hour? Almost certainly; for by now the whole Moon, and the whole Earth, must know of his predicament. Perhaps they were searching for him with radar and telescope, but they would have little time to find him. Within seconds, the unknown city had dropped out of sight, and he was once more alone above Farside.

It was impossible to judge his altitude above the blank emptiness speeding below, for there was no sense of scale or perspective. Sometimes it seemed that he could reach out and touch the darkness across which he was racing; yet he knew that in reality it must still be many miles beneath him. But he also knew that he was still descending, and that at any moment one of the crater walls or mountain peaks that strained invisibly toward him might claw him from the sky.

In the darkness somewhere ahead was the final obstacle—the hazard he feared most of all. Across the heart of Farside, spanning the equator from north to south in a wall more than a thousand miles long, lay the Soviet Range. He had been a boy when it was discovered, back in 1959, and could still remember his excitement when he had seen the first smudged photographs from Lunik III. He could never have dreamed that one day he would be flying toward those same mountains, waiting for them to decide his fate.

The first eruption of dawn took him completely by surprise. Light exploded ahead of him, leaping from peak to peak until the whole arc of the horizon was limned with flame. He was hurtling out of the lunar night, directly into the face of the Sun. At least he would not die in darkness, but the greatest danger was yet to come. For now he was almost back where he had started, nearing the lowest point of his orbit. He glanced at the suit chronometer, and saw that five full hours had now passed. Within minutes, he would hit the Moon—or skim it and pass safely out into space.

As far as he could judge, he was less than twenty miles above the surface, and he was still descending, though very slowly now. Beneath him, the long shadows of the lunar dawn were daggers of darkness, stabbing toward the night land. The steeply slanting sunlight exaggerated every rise in the ground, making even the smallest hills appear to be mountains. And now, unmistakably, the land ahead was rising, wrinkling into the foothills of the Soviet Range. More than a hundred miles away, but approaching at a mile a second, a wave of rock was climbing from the face of the Moon. There was nothing he could do to avoid it; his path was fixed and unalterable. All that could be done had already been done, two and a half hours ago.

It was not enough. He was not going to rise above these mountains; they were rising above him.

Now he regretted his failure to make that second call to the woman who was still waiting, a quarter of a million miles away. Yet perhaps it was just as well, for there had been nothing more to say.

Other voices were calling in the space around him, as he came once more within range of Launch Control. They waxed and waned as he flashed through the radio shadow of the mountains; they were talking about him, but the fact scarcely registered on him. He listened with an impersonal interest, as if to messages from some remote point of space or time, of no concern to him. Once he heard Van Kessel's voice say, quite distinctly: "Tell *Callisto*'s skipper we'll give him an intercept orbit as soon as we know that Leyland's past perigee. Rendezvous time should be one hour five minutes from now." I hate to disappoint you, thought Cliff, but that's one appointment I'll never keep.

Now the wall of rock was only fifty miles away, and each time he spun helplessly in space it came ten miles closer. There was no room for optimism now, as he sped more swiftly than a rifle bullet toward that implacable barrier. This was the end, and suddenly it became of great importance to know whether he would meet it face first, with open eyes, or with his back turned, like a coward.

No memories of his past life flashed through Cliff's mind as he counted the seconds that remained. The swiftly unrolling moonscape rotated beneath him, every detail sharp and clear in the harsh light of dawn. Now he was turned away from the onrushing mountains, looking back on the path he had traveled, the path that should have led to Earth. No more than three of his ten-second days were left to him.

And then the moonscape exploded into silent flame. A light as fierce as that of the sun banished the long shadows, struck fire from the peaks and craters spread below. It lasted for only a fraction of a second, and had faded completely before he had turned toward its source.

Directly ahead of him, only twenty miles away, a vast cloud of dust was expanding toward the stars. It was as if a volcano had erupted in the Soviet Range—but that, of course, was impossible. Equally absurd was Cliff's second thought—that by some fantastic feat of organization and logistics the Farside Engineering Division had blasted away the obstacle in his path.

For it was gone. A huge, crescent-shaped bite had been taken out of the approaching skyline; rocks and debris were still rising from a crater that had not existed five seconds ago. Only the energy of an atomic bomb, exploded at precisely the right moment in his path, could have wrought such a miracle. And Cliff did not believe in miracles.

He had made another complete revolution, and was almost upon the mountains, when he remembered that, all this while, there had been a cosmic bulldozer moving invisibly ahead of him. The kinetic energy of the abandoned capsule—a thousand tons, traveling at over a mile a second—was quite sufficient to have blasted the gap through which he was now racing. The impact of the man-made meteor must have jolted the whole of Farside.

His luck held to the end. There was brief pitter-patter of dust particles against his suit, and he caught a blurred glimpse of glowing rocks and swiftly dispersing smoke clouds flashing beneath him. (How strange to see a cloud upon the Moon!) Then he was through the mountains, with nothing ahead but blessed empty sky.

Somewhere up there, an hour in the future along his second orbit, *Callisto* would be moving to meet him. But there was no hurry now; he had escaped from the maelstrom. For better or for worse, he had been granted the gift of life.

There was the launching track, a few miles to the right of his path; it looked like a hairline scribed across the face of the Moon. In a few moments he would be within radio range. Now, with thankfulness and joy, he could make that second call to Earth, to the woman who was still waiting in the African night.

May 1962

The Shining Ones

When the switchboard said that the Soviet Embassy was on the line, my first reaction was: "Good—another job!" But the moment I heard Goncharov's voice, I knew there was trouble.

"Klaus? This is Mikhail. Can you come over at once? It's very urgent, and I can't talk on the phone."

I worried all the way to the Embassy, marshaling my defenses in case anything had gone wrong at our end. But I could think of nothing; at the moment, we had no outstanding contracts with the Russians. The last job had been completed six months ago, on time, and to their entire satisfaction.

Well, they were not satisfied with it now, as I discovered quickly enough. Mikhail Goncharov, the Commercial Attaché, was an old friend of mine; he told me all he knew, but it was not much.

"We've just had an urgent cable from Ceylon," he said. "They want you out there immediately. There's serious trouble at the hydrothermal project."

"What sort of trouble?" I asked. I knew at once, of course, that it would be the deep end, for that was the only part of the installation that had concerned us. The Russians themselves had done all the work on land, but they had had to call on us to fix those grids three thousand feet down in the Indian Ocean. There is no other firm in the world that can live up to our motto: ANY JOB, ANY DEPTH.

"All I know," said Mikhail, "is that the site engineers report a complete breakdown, that the Prime Minister of Ceylon is opening the plant three weeks from now, and that Moscow will be very, very unhappy if it's not working then."

My mind went rapidly through the penalty clauses in our

contract. The firm seemed to be covered, because the client had signed the take-over certificate, thereby admitting that the job was up to specification. However, it was not as simple as that; if negligence on our part was proved, we might be safe from legal action—but it would be very bad for business. And it would be even worse for me, personally; for I had been project supervisor in Trinco Deep.

Don't call me a diver, please; I hate the name. I'm a deep-sea engineer, and I use diving gear about as often as an airman uses a parachute. Most of my work is done with TV and remote-controlled robots. When I do have to go down myself, I'm inside a minisub with external manipulators. We call it a lobster, because of its claws; the standard model works down to five thousand feet, but there are special versions that will operate at the bottom of the Marianas Trench. I've never been there myself, but will be glad to quote terms if you're interested. At a rough estimate, it will cost you a dollar a foot plus a thousand an hour on the job itself.

I realized that the Russians meant business when Mikhail said that a jet was waiting at Zurich, and could I be at the airport within two hours?

"Look," I said, "I can't do a thing without equipment—and the gear needed even for an inspection weighs tons. Besides, it's all at Spezia."

"I know," Mikhail answered implacably. "We'll have another jet transport there. Cable from Ceylon as soon as you know what you want: it will be on the site within twelve hours. But please don't talk to anyone about this; we prefer to keep our problems to ourselves."

I agreed with this, for it was my problem, too. As I left the office, Mikhail pointed to the wall calendar, said "Three weeks," and ran his finger around his throat. And I knew he wasn't thinking of *his* neck.

Two hours later I was climbing over the Alps, saying good-by to the family by radio, and wondering why, like every other sensible Swiss, I hadn't become a banker or gone into the watch business. It was all the fault of the Picards and Hannes

Keller, I told myself moodily: why did they have to start this deep-sea tradition, in Switzerland of all countries? Then I settled down to sleep, knowing that I would have little enough in the days to come.

We landed at Trincomalee just after dawn, and the huge, complex harbor—whose geography I've never quite mastered—was a maze of capes, islands, interconnecting waterways, and basins large enough to hold all the navies of the world. I could see the big white control building, in a somewhat flamboyant architectural style, on a headland overlooking the Indian Ocean. The site was pure propaganda—though of course if I'd been Russian I'd have called it "public relations."

Not that I really blamed my clients; they had good reason to be proud of this, the most ambitious attempt yet made to harness the thermal energy of the sea. It was not the first attempt. There had been an unsuccessful one by the French scientist Georges Claude in the 1930's, and a much bigger one at Abidjan, on the west coast of Africa, in the 1950's.

All these projects depended on the same surprising fact: even in the tropics the sea a mile down is almost at freezing point. Where billions of tons of water are concerned, this temperature difference represents a colossal amount of energy—and a fine challenge to the engineers of power-starved countries.

Claude and his successors had tried to tap this energy with low-pressure steam engines; the Russians had used a much simpler and more direct method. For over a hundred years it had been known that electric currents flow in many materials if one end is heated and the other cooled, and ever since the 1940's Russian scientists had been working to put this "thermoelectric" effect to practical use. Their earliest devices had not been very efficient—though good enough to power thousands of radios by the heat of kerosene lamps. But in 1974 they had made a big, and still-secret, break-through. Though I fixed the power elements at the cold end of the system, I never really saw them; they were completely hidden in anticorrosive paint. All I know is that they formed a big grid, like lots of old-fashioned steam radiators bolted together.

I recognized most of the faces in the little crowd waiting on the Trinco airstrip; friends or enemies, they all seemed glad to see me—especially Chief Engineer Shapiro.

"Well, Lev," I said, as we drove out in the station wagon, "what's the trouble?"

"We don't know," he said frankly. "It's your job to find out—and to put it right."

"Well, what *happened?*"

"Everything worked perfectly up to the full-power tests," he answered. "Output was within five per cent of estimate until 0134 Tuesday morning." He grimaced; obviously that time was engraved on his heart. "Then the voltage started to fluctuate violently, so we cut the load and watched the meters. I thought that some idiot of a skipper had hooked the cables —you know the trouble we've taken to avoid *that* happening—so we switched on the searchlights and looked out to sea. There wasn't a ship in sight. Anyway, who would have tried to anchor just *outside* the harbor on a clear, calm night?

"There was nothing we could do except watch the instruments and keep testing; I'll show you all the graphs when we get to the office. After four minutes everything went open circuit. We can locate the break exactly, of course—and it's in the deepest part, right at the grid. It *would* be there, and not at *this* end of the system," he added gloomily, pointing out the window.

We were just driving past the Solar Pond—the equivalent of the boiler in a conventional heat engine. This was an idea that the Russians had borrowed from the Israelis. It was simply a shallow lake, blackened at the bottom, holding a concentrated solution of brine. It acts as a very efficient heat trap, and the sun's rays bring the liquid up to almost two hundred degrees Fahrenheit. Submerged in it were the "hot" grids of the thermoelectric system, every inch of two fathoms down. Massive cables connected them to my department, a hundred and fifty degrees colder and three thousand feet lower, in the undersea canyon that comes to the very entrance of Trinco harbor.

"I suppose you checked for earthquakes?" I asked, not very hopefully.

"Of course. There was nothing on the seismograph."

"What about whales? I warned you that they might give trouble."

More than a year ago, when the main conductors were being run out to sea, I'd told the engineers about the drowned sperm whale found entangled in a telegraph cable half a mile down off South America. About a dozen similar cases are known—but ours, it seemed, was not one of them.

"That was the second thing we thought of," answered Shapiro. "We got on to the Fisheries Department, the Navy, and the Air Force. No whales anywhere along the coast."

It was at that point that I stopped theorizing, because I overheard something that made me a little uncomfortable. Like all Swiss, I'm good at languages, and have picked up a fair amount of Russian. There was no need to be much of a linguist, however, to recognize the word *sabotash.*

It was spoken by Dimitri Karpukhin, the political adviser on the project. I didn't like him; nor did the engineers, who sometimes went out of their way to be rude to him. One of the old-style Communists who had never quite escaped from the shadow of Stalin, he was suspicious of everything outside the Soviet Union, and most of the things inside it. Sabotage was just the explanation that would appeal to him.

There were, of course, a great many people who would not exactly be brokenhearted if the Trinco Power Project failed. Politically, the prestige of the USSR was committed; economically, billions were involved, for if hydrothermal plants proved a success, they might compete with oil, coal, water power, and, especially, nuclear energy.

Yet I could not really believe in sabotage; after all, the Cold War was over. It was just possible that someone had made a clumsy attempt to grab a sample of the grid, but even this seemed unlikely. I could count on my fingers the number of people in the world who could tackle such a job—and half of them were on my payroll.

The underwater TV camera arrived that same evening, and by working all through the night we had cameras, monitors, and over a mile of coaxial cable loaded aboard a launch. As we pulled out of the harbor, I thought I saw a familiar figure standing on the jetty, but it was too far to be certain and I had other things on my mind. If you must know, I am not a good sailor; I am only really happy *underneath* the sea.

We took a careful fix on the Round Island lighthouse and stationed ourselves directly above the grid. The self-propelled camera, looking like a midget bathyscape, went over the side; as we watched the monitors, we went with it in spirit.

The water was extremely clear, and extremely empty, but as we neared the bottom there were a few signs of life. A small shark came and stared at us. Then a pulsating blob of jelly went drifting by, followed by a thing like a big spider, with hundreds of hairy legs tangling and twisting together. At last the sloping canyon wall swam into view. We were right on target, for there were the thick cables running down into the depths, just as I had seen them when I made the final check of the installation six months ago.

I turned on the low-powered jets and let the camera drift down the power cables. They seemed in perfect condition, still firmly anchored by the pitons we had driven into the rock. It was not until I came to the grid itself that there was any sign of trouble.

Have you ever seen the radiator grille of a car after it's run into a lamppost? Well, one section of the grid looked very much like that. Something had battered it in, as if a madman had gone to work on it with a sledgehammer.

There were gasps of astonishment and anger from the people looking over my shoulder. I heard *sabotash* muttered again, and for the first time began to take it seriously. The only other explanation that made sense was a falling boulder, but the slopes of the canyon had been carefully checked against this very possibility.

Whatever the cause, the damaged grid had to be replaced.

That could not be done until my lobster—all twenty tons of it—had been flown out from the Spezia dockyard where it was kept between jobs.

"Well," said Shapiro, when I had finished my visual inspection and photographed the sorry spectacle on the screen, "how long will it take?"

I refused to commit myself. The first thing I ever learned in the underwater business is that no job turns out as you expect. Cost and time estimates can never be firm because it's not until you're halfway through a contract that you know exactly what you're up against.

My private guess was three days. So I said: "If everything goes well, it shouldn't take more than a week."

Shapiro groaned. "Can't you do it quicker?"

"I won't tempt fate by making rash promises. Anyway, that still gives you two weeks before your deadline."

He had to be content with that, though he kept nagging at me all the way back into the harbor. When we got there, he had something else to think about.

"Morning, Joe," I said to the man who was still waiting patiently on the jetty. "I thought I recognized you on the way out. What are *you* doing here?"

"I was going to ask you the same question."

"You'd better speak to my boss. Chief Engineer Shapiro, meet Joe Watkins, science correspondent of *Time*."

Lev's response was not exactly cordial. Normally, there was nothing he liked better than talking to newsmen, who arrived at the rate of about one a week. Now, as the target date approached, they would be flying in from all directions. Including, of course, Russia. And at the present moment Tass would be just as unwelcome as *Time*.

It was amusing to see how Karpukhin took charge of the situation. From that moment, Joe had permanently attached to him as guide, philosopher, and drinking companion a smooth young public-relations type named Sergei Markov. Despite all Joe's efforts, the two were inseparable. In the middle of the afternoon, weary after a long conference in

Shapiro's office, I caught up with them for a belated lunch at the government resthouse.

"What's going on here, Klaus?" Joe asked pathetically. "I smell trouble, but no one will admit anything."

I toyed with my curry, trying to separate the bits that were safe from those that would take off the top of my head.

"You can't expect me to discuss a client's affairs," I answered.

"You were talkative enough," Joe reminded me, "when you were doing the survey for the Gibraltar Dam."

"Well, yes," I admitted. "And I appreciate the write-up you gave me. But this time there are trade secrets involved. I'm—ah—making some last-minute adjustments to improve the efficiency of the system."

And that, of course, was the truth; for I was indeed hoping to raise the efficiency of the system from its present value of exactly zero.

"Hmm," said Joe sarcastically. "Thank you very much."

"Anyway," I said, trying to head him off, "what's *your* latest crackbrained theory?"

For a highly competent science writer, Joe has an odd liking for the bizarre and the improbable. Perhaps it's a form of escapism; I happen to know that he also writes science fiction, though this is a well-kept secret from his employers. He has a sneaking fondness for poltergeists and ESP and flying saucers, but lost continents are his real specialty.

"I *am* working on a couple of ideas," he admitted. "They cropped up when I was doing the research on this story."

"Go on," I said, not daring to look up from the analysis of my curry.

"The other day I came across a very old map—Ptolemy's, if you're interested—of Ceylon. It reminded me of another old map in my collection, and I turned it up. There was the same central mountain, the same arrangement of rivers flowing to the sea. But *this* was a map of Atlantis."

"Oh, no!" I groaned. "Last time we met, you convinced me that Atlantis was the western Mediterranean basin."

Joe gave his engaging grin.

"I could be wrong, couldn't I? Anyway, I've a much more striking piece of evidence. What's the old national name for Ceylon—and the modern Sinhalese one, for that matter?"

I thought for a second, then exclaimed: "Good Lord! Why, Lanka, of course. Lanka—Atlantis." I rolled the names off my tongue.

"Precisely," said Joe. "But two clues, however striking, don't make a full-fledged theory; and that's as far as I've got at the moment."

"Too bad," I said, genuinely disappointed. "And your other project?"

"This will really make you sit up," Joe answered smugly. He reached into the battered briefcase he always carried and pulled out a bundle of papers.

"This happened only one hundred and eighty miles from here, and just over a century ago. The source of my information, you'll note, is about the best there is."

He handed me a photostat, and I saw that it was a page of the London *Times* for July 4, 1874. I started to read without much enthusiasm, for Joe was always producing bits of ancient newspapers, but my apathy did not last for long.

Briefly—I'd like to give the whole thing, but if you want more details your local library can dial you a facsimile in ten seconds—the clipping described how the one-hundred-and-fifty-ton schooner *Pearl* left Ceylon in early May 1874 and then fell becalmed in the Bay of Bengal. On May 10, just before nightfall, an enormous squid surfaced half a mile from the schooner, whose captain foolishly opened fire on it with his rifle.

The squid swam straight for the *Pearl,* grabbed the masts with its arms, and pulled the vessel over on her side. She sank within seconds, taking two of her crew with her. The others were rescued only by the lucky chance that the P. and O. steamer *Strathowen* was in sight and had witnessed the incident herself.

"Well," said Joe, when I'd read through it for the second time, "what do you think?"

"I don't believe in sea monsters."

"The London *Times*," Joe answered, "is not prone to sensational journalism. And giant squids exist, though the biggest *we* know about are feeble, flabby beasts and don't weigh more than a ton, even when they have arms forty feet long."

"So? An animal like that couldn't capsize a hundred-and-fifty-ton schooner."

"True—but there's a lot of evidence that the so-called *giant* squid is merely a large squid. There may be decapods in the sea that really are giants. Why, only a year after the *Pearl* incident, a sperm whale off the coast of Brazil was seen struggling inside gigantic coils which finally *dragged it down into the sea*. You'll find the incident described in the *Illustrated London News* for November 20, 1875. And then, of course, there's that chapter in *Moby-Dick*. . . ."

"What chapter?"

"Why, the one called 'Squid.' We know that Melville was a very careful observer—but here he really lets himself go. He describes a calm day when a great white mass rose out of the sea 'like a snow-slide, new slid from the hills.' And this happened here in the Indian Ocean, perhaps a thousand miles south of the *Pearl* incident. Weather conditions were identical, please note.

"What the men of the *Pequod* saw floating on the water—I know this passage by heart, I've studied it so carefully—was a 'vast pulpy mass, furlongs in length and breadth, of a glancing cream-color, innumerable long arms radiating from its centre, curling and twisting like a nest of anacondas.' "

"Just a minute," said Sergei, who had been listening to all this with rapt attention. "What's a furlong?"

Joe looked slightly embarrassed.

"Actually, it's an eighth of a mile—six hundred and sixty feet." He raised his hand to stop our incredulous laughter. "Oh, I'm sure Melville didn't mean that *literally*. But here was a man who met sperm whales every day, groping for a unit of length to describe something a lot bigger. So he automatically jumped from fathoms to furlongs. That's my theory, anyway."

I pushed away the remaining untouchable portions of my curry.

"If you think you've scared me out of my job," I said, "you've failed miserably. But I promise you this—when I do meet a giant squid, I'll snip off a tentacle and bring it back as a souvenir."

Twenty-four hours later I was out there in the lobster, sinking slowly down toward the damaged grid. There was no way in which the operation could be kept secret, and Joe was an interested spectator from a nearby launch. That was the Russians' problem, not mine; I had suggested to Shapiro that they take him into their confidence, but this, of course, was vetoed by Karpukhin's suspicious Slavic mind. One could almost see him thinking: Just *why* should an American reporter turn up at this moment? And ignoring the obvious answer that Trincomalee was now big news.

There is nothing in the least exciting or glamorous about deep-water operations—if they're done properly. Excitement means lack of foresight, and that means incompetence. The incompetent do not last long in my business, nor do those who crave excitement. I went about my job with all the pent-up emotion of a plumber dealing with a leaking faucet.

The grids had been designed for easy maintenance, since sooner or later they would have to be replaced. Luckily, none of the threads had been damaged, and the securing nuts came off easily when gripped with the power wrench. Then I switched control to the heavy-duty claws, and lifted out the damaged grid without the slightest difficulty.

It's bad tactics to hurry an underwater operation. If you try to do too much at once, you are liable to make mistakes. And if things go smoothly and you finish in a day a job you said would take a week, the client feels he hasn't had his money's worth. Though I was sure I could replace the grid that same afternoon, I followed the damaged unit up to the surface and closed shop for the day.

The thermoelement was rushed off for an autopsy, and I

spent the rest of the evening hiding from Joe. Trinco is a small town, but I managed to keep out of his way by visiting the local cinema, where I sat through several hours of an interminable Tamil movie in which three successive generations suffered identical domestic crises of mistaken identity, drunkenness, desertion, death, and insanity, all in Technicolor and with the sound track turned full up.

The next morning, despite a mild headache, I was at the site soon after dawn. (So was Joe, and so was Sergei, all set for a quiet day's fishing.) I cheerfully waved to them as I climbed into the lobster, and the tender's crane lowered me over the side. Over the other side, where Joe couldn't see it, went the replacement grid. A few fathoms down I lifted it out of the hoist and carried it to the bottom of Trinco Deep, where, without any trouble, it was installed by the middle of the afternoon. Before I surfaced again, the lock nuts had been secured, the conductors spot-welded, and the engineers on shore had completed their continuity tests. By the time I was back on deck, the system was under load once more, everything was back to normal, and even Karpukhin was smiling —except when he stopped to ask himself the question that no one had yet been able to answer.

I still clung to the falling-boulder theory—for want of a better. And I hoped that the Russians would accept it, so that we could stop this silly cloak-and-dagger business with Joe.

No such luck, I realized, when both Shapiro and Karpukhin came to see me with very long faces.

"Klaus," said Lev, "we want you to go down again."

"It's your money," I replied. "But what do you want me to do?"

"We've examined the damaged grid, and there's a section of the thermoelement missing. Dimitri thinks that—someone —has deliberately broken it off and carried it away."

"Then they did a damn clumsy job," I answered. "I can promise you it wasn't one of *my* men."

It was risky to make such jokes around Karpukhin, and

no one was at all amused. Not even me; for by this time I was beginning to think that he had something.

The sun was setting when I began my last dive into Trinco Deep, but the end of day has no meaning down there. I fell for two thousand feet with no lights, because I like to watch the luminous creatures of the sea, as they flash and flicker in the darkness, sometimes exploding like rockets just outside the observation window. In this open water, there was no danger of a collision; in any case, I had the panoramic sonar scan running, and that gave far better warning than my eyes.

At four hundred fathoms, I knew that something was wrong. The bottom was coming into view on the vertical sounder—but it was approaching much too slowly. My rate of descent was far too slow. I could increase it easily enough by flooding another buoyancy tank—but I hesitated to do so. In my business, anything out of the ordinary needs an explanation; three times I have saved my life by waiting until I had one.

The thermometer gave me the answer. The temperature outside was five degrees higher than it should have been, and I am sorry to say that it took me several seconds to realize why.

Only a few hundred feet below me, the repaired grid was now running at full power, pouring out megawatts of heat as it tried to equalize the temperature difference between Trinco Deep and the Solar Pond up there on land. It wouldn't succeed, of course; but in the attempt it was generating electricity —and I was being swept upward in the geyser of warm water that was an incidental by-product.

When I finally reached the grid, it was quite difficult to keep the lobster in position against the upwelling current, and I began to sweat uncomfortably as the heat penetrated into the cabin. Being too hot on the sea bed was a novel experience; so also was the miragelike vision caused by the ascending water, which made my searchlights dance and tremble over the rock face I was exploring.

You must picture me, lights ablaze in that five-hundred-fathom darkness, moving slowly down the slope of the canyon, which at this spot was about as steep as the roof of a house. The missing element—*if* it was still around—could not have fallen very far before coming to rest. I would find it in ten minutes, or not at all.

After an hour's searching, I had turned up several broken light bulbs (it's astonishing how many get thrown overboard from ships—the sea beds of the world are covered with them), an empty beer bottle (same comment), and a brand-new boot. That was the last thing I found, for then I discovered that I was no longer alone.

I never switch off the sonar scan, and even when I'm not moving I always glance at the screen about once a minute to check the general situation. The situation now was that a large object—at least the size of the lobster—was approaching from the north. When I spotted it, the range was about five hundred feet and closing slowly. I switched off my lights, cut the jets I had been running at low power to hold me in the turbulent water, and drifted with the current.

Though I was tempted to call Shapiro and report that I had company, I decided to wait for more information. There were only three nations with depth ships that could operate at this level, and I was on excellent terms with all of them. It would never do to be too hasty, and to get myself involved in unnecessary political complications.

Though I felt blind without the sonar, I did not wish to advertise my presence, so I reluctantly switched it off and relied on my eyes. Anyone working at this depth would have to use lights, and I'd see them coming long before they could see me. So I waited in the hot, silent little cabin, straining my eyes into the darkness, tense and alert but not particularly worried.

First there was a dim glow, at an indefinite distance. It grew bigger and brighter, yet refused to shape itself into any pattern that my mind could recognize. The diffuse glow concentrated into myriad spots, until it seemed that a constellation was sailing toward me. Thus might the rising star clouds of the galaxy appear, from some world close to the heart of the Milky Way.

It is not true that men are frightened of the unknown; they can be frightened only of the known, the already experienced. I could not imagine what was approaching, but no creature of the sea could touch me inside six inches of good Swiss armor plate.

The thing was almost upon me, glowing with the light of its own creation, when it split into two separate clouds. Slowly they came into focus—not of my eyes, but of my understanding—and I knew that beauty and terror were rising toward me out of the abyss.

The terror came first, when I saw that the approaching beasts were squids, and all Joe's tales reverberated in my brain. Then, with a considerable sense of letdown, I realized that they were only about twenty feet long—little larger than the lobster, and a mere fraction of its weight. They could do me no harm. And quite apart from that, their indescribable beauty robbed them of all menace.

This sounds ridiculous, but it is true. In my travels I have seen most of the animals of this world, but none to match the luminous apparitions floating before me now. The colored lights that pulsed and danced along their bodies made them seem clothed with jewels, never the same for two seconds at a time. There were patches that glowed a brilliant blue, like flickering mercury arcs, then changed almost instantly to burning neon red. The tentacles seemed strings of luminous beads, trailing through the water—or the lamps along a superhighway, when you look down upon it from the air at night. Barely visible against this background glow were the enormous eyes, uncannily human and intelligent, each surrounded by a diadem of shining pearls.

I am sorry, but that is the best I can do. Only the movie camera could do justice to these living kaleidoscopes. I do not know how long I watched them, so entranced by their luminous beauty that I had almost forgotten my mission. That those delicate, whiplash tentacles could not possibly have broken the grid was already obvious. Yet the presence of these creatures here was, to say the least, very curious. Karpukhin would have called it suspicious.

I was about to call the surface when I saw something incredible. It had been before my eyes all the time, but I had not realized it until now.

The squids were talking to each other.

Those glowing, evanescent patterns were not coming and going at random. They were as meaningful, I was suddenly sure, as the illuminated signs of Broadway or Piccadilly. Every few seconds there was an image that almost made sense, but it vanished before I could interpret it. I knew, of course, that even the common octopus shows its emotions with lightning-fast color changes—but this was something of a much higher order. It was real communication: here were two living electric signs, flashing messages to one another.

When I saw an unmistakable picture of the lobster, my last doubts vanished. Though I am no scientist, at that moment I shared the feelings of a Newton or an Einstein at some moment of revelation. *This* would make me famous. . . .

Then the picture changed—in a most curious manner. There was the lobster again, but rather smaller. And there beside it, much smaller still, were two peculiar objects. Each consisted of a pair of black dots surrounded by a pattern of ten radiating lines.

Just now I said that we Swiss are good at languages. However, it required little intelligence to deduce that this was a formalized squid's-eye-view of itself, and that what I was seeing was a crude sketch of the situation. But why the absurdly small size of the squids?

I had no time to puzzle that out before there was another change. A third squid symbol appeared on the living screen—and this one was enormous, completely dwarfing the others. The message shone there in the eternal night for a few seconds. Then the creature bearing it shot off at incredible speed, and left me alone with its companion.

Now the meaning was all too obvious. "My God!" I said to

myself. "They feel they can't handle me. They've gone to fetch Big Brother."

And of Big Brother's capabilities, I already had better evidence than Joe Watkins, for all his research and newspaper clippings.

That was the point—you won't be surprised to hear—when I decided not to linger. But before I went, I thought I would try some talking myself.

After hanging here in darkness for so long, I had forgotten the power of my lights. They hurt my eyes, and must have been agonizing to the unfortunate squid. Transfixed by that intolerable glare, its own illumination utterly quenched, it lost all its beauty, becoming no more than a pallid bag of jelly with two black buttons for eyes. For a moment it seemed paralyzed by the shock; then it darted after its companion, while I soared upward to a world that could never be the same again.

"I've found your saboteur," I told Karpukhin, when they opened the hatch of the lobster. "If you want to know all about him, ask Joe Watkins."

I let Dimitri sweat over that for a few seconds, while I enjoyed his expression. Then I gave my slightly edited report. I implied—without actually saying so—that the squids I'd met were powerful enough to have done all the damage; and I said nothing about the conversation I'd overseen. That would only cause incredulity. Besides, I wanted time to think matters over, and to tidy up the loose ends—if I could.

Joe has been a great help, though he still knows no more than the Russians. He's told me what wonderfully developed nervous systems squids possess, and has explained how some of them can change their appearance in a flash through instantaneous three-color printing, thanks to the extraordinary network of "chromophores" covering their bodies. Presumably this evolved for camouflage; but it seems natural—even inevitable—that it should develop into a communication system.

But there's one thing that worries Joe.

"What were they *doing* around the grid?" he keeps asking

me plaintively. "They're cold-blooded invertebrates. You'd expect them to dislike heat as much as they object to light."

That puzzles Joe; but it doesn't puzzle me. Indeed, I think it's the key to the whole mystery.

Those squids, I'm now certain, are in Trinco Deep for the same reason that there are men at the South Pole—or on the Moon. Pure scientific curiosity has drawn them from their icy home, to investigate this geyser of hot water welling from the sides of the canyon. Here is a strange and inexplicable phenomenon—possibly one that menaces their way of life. So they have summoned their giant cousin (servant? slave!) to bring them a sample for study. I cannot believe that they have a hope of understanding it; after all, no scientist on earth could have done so as little as a century ago. But they are trying; and that is what matters.

Tomorrow, we begin our countermeasures. I go back into Trinco Deep to fix the great lights that Shapiro hopes will keep the squids at bay. But how long will that ruse work, if intelligence is dawning in the deep?

As I dictate this, I'm sitting here below the ancient battlements of Fort Frederick, watching the Moon come up over the Indian Ocean. If everything goes well, this will serve as the opening of the book that Joe has been badgering me to write. If it doesn't—then hello, Joe, I'm talking to *you* now. Please edit this for publication, in any way you think fit, and my apologies to you and Lev for not giving you all the facts before. Now you'll understand why.

Whatever happens, please remember this: they are beautiful, wonderful creatures; try to come to terms with them if you can.

To: Ministry of Power, Moscow
From: Lev Shapiro, Chief Engineer, Trincomalee Thermoelectric Power Project

Herewith the complete transcript of the tape recording found among Herr Klaus Muller's effects after his last dive.

We are much indebted to Mr. Joe Watkins, of *Time,* for assistance on several points.

You will recall that Herr Muller's last intelligible message was directed to Mr. Watkins and ran as follows: "Joe! You were right about Melville! The thing is absolutely gigan—"

December 1962

The Wind from the Sun

The enormous disc of sail strained at its rigging, already filled with the wind that blew between the worlds. In three minutes the race would begin, yet now John Merton felt more relaxed, more at peace, than at any time for the past year. Whatever happened when the Commodore gave the starting signal, whether *Diana* carried him to victory or defeat, he had achieved his ambition. After a lifetime spent designing ships for others, now he would sail his own.

"T minus two minutes," said the cabin radio. "Please confirm your readiness."

One by one, the other skippers answered. Merton recognized all the voices—some tense, some calm—for they were the voices of his friends and rivals. On the four inhabited worlds, there were scarcely twenty men who could sail a sun yacht; and they were all here, on the starting line or aboard the escort vessels, orbiting twenty-two thousand miles above the equator.

"Number One—*Gossamer*—ready to go."

"Number Two—*Santa Maria*—all O.K."

"Number Three—*Sunbeam*—O.K."

"Number Four—*Woomera*—all systems go."

Merton smiled at that last echo from the early, primitive days of astronautics. But it had become part of the tradition of space; and there were times when a man needed to evoke the shades of those who had gone before him to the stars.

"Number Five—*Lebedev*—we're ready."

"Number Six—*Arachne*—O.K."

Now it was his turn, at the end of the line; strange to think that the words he was speaking in this tiny cabin were being heard by at least five billion people.

"Number Seven—*Diana*—ready to start."

"One through Seven acknowledged," answered that impersonal voice from the judge's launch. "Now T minus one minute."

Merton scarcely heard it. For the last time, he was checking the tension in the rigging. The needles of all the dynamometers were steady; the immense sail was taut, its mirror surface sparkling and glittering gloriously in the sun.

To Merton, floating weightless at the periscope, it seemed to fill the sky. As well it might—for out there were fifty million square feet of sail, linked to his capsule by almost a hundred miles of rigging. All the canvas of all the tea clippers that had once raced like clouds across the China seas, sewn into one gigantic sheet, could not match the single sail that *Diana* had spread beneath the sun. Yet it was little more substantial than a soap bubble; that two square miles of aluminized plastic was only a few millionths of an inch thick.

"T minus ten seconds. All recording cameras ON."

Something so huge, yet so frail, was hard for the mind to grasp. And it was harder still to realize that this fragile mirror could tow him free of Earth merely by the power of the sunlight it would trap.

". . . five, four, three, two, one, CUT!"

Seven knife blades sliced through seven thin lines tethering the yachts to the mother ships that had assembled and serviced them. Until this moment, all had been circling Earth together in a rigidly held formation, but now the yachts would begin to disperse, like dandelion seeds drifting before the breeze. And the winner would be the one that first drifted past the Moon.

Aboard *Diana,* nothing seemed to be happening. But Merton knew better. Though his body could feel no thrust, the instrument board told him that he was now accelerating at almost one thousandth of a gravity. For a rocket, that figure would have been ludicrous—but this was the first time any solar yacht had ever attained it. *Diana*'s design was sound; the vast sail was living up to his calculations. At this rate, two circuits of the Earth would build up his speed to escape velocity, and then he could head out for the Moon, with the full force of the Sun behind him.

The full force of the Sun . . . He smiled wryly, remembering all his attempts to explain solar sailing to those lecture audiences back on Earth. That had been the only way he could raise money, in those early days. He might be Chief Designer of Cosmodyne Corporation, with a whole string of successful spaceships to his credit, but his firm had not been exactly enthusiastic about his hobby.

"Hold your hands out to the Sun," he'd said. "What do you feel? Heat, of course. But there's pressure as well—though you've never noticed it, because it's so tiny. Over the area of your hands, it comes to only about a millionth of an ounce.

"But out in space, even a pressure as small as that can be important, for it's acting all the time, hour after hour, day after day. Unlike rocket fuel, it's free and unlimited. If we want to, we can use it. We can build sails to catch the radiation blowing from the Sun."

At that point, he would pull out a few square yards of sail material and toss it toward the audience. The silvery film would coil and twist like smoke, then drift slowly to the ceiling in the hot-air currents.

"You can see how light it is," he'd continue. "A square mile weighs only a ton, and can collect five pounds of radiation pressure. So it will start moving—and we can let it tow us along, if we attach rigging to it.

"Of course, its acceleration will be tiny—about a thousandth of a g. That doesn't seem much, but let's see what it means.

"It means that in the first second, we'll move about a fifth of an inch. I suppose a healthy snail could do better than that. But after a minute, we've covered sixty feet, and will be doing just over a mile an hour. That's not bad, for something driven by pure sunlight! After an hour, we're forty miles from our starting point, and will be moving at eighty miles an hour. Please remember that in space there's no friction; so once you start anything moving, it will keep going forever. You'll be surprised when I tell you what our thousandth-of-a-g sailboat will be doing at the end of a day's run: *almost two thousand miles an hour!* If it starts from orbit—as it has to, of course—it can reach escape velocity in a couple of days. And all without burning a single drop of fuel!"

Well, he'd convinced them, and in the end he'd even convinced Cosmodyne. Over the last twenty years, a new sport had come into being. It had been called the sport of billionaires, and that was true. But it was beginning to pay for itself in terms of publicity and TV coverage. The prestige of four continents and two worlds was riding on this race, and it had the biggest audience in history.

Diana had made a good start; time to take a look at the opposition. Moving very gently—though there were shock absorbers between the control capsule and the delicate rigging, he was determined to run no risks—Merton stationed himself at the periscope.

There they were, looking like strange silver flowers planted in the dark fields of space. The nearest, South America's *Santa Maria,* was only fifty miles away; it bore a close resemblance to a boy's kite, but a kite more than a mile on a side. Farther away, the University of Astrograd's *Lebedev* looked like a Maltese cross; the sails that formed the four arms could apparently be tilted for steering purposes. In contrast, the Federation of Australasia's *Woomera* was a simple parachute, four miles in circumference. General Spacecraft's *Arachne,* as its name suggested, looked like a spider web, and had been built on the same principles, by robot shuttles spiraling out from a central point. Eurospace Corporation's *Gossamer* was an identical design, on a slightly smaller scale. And the Republic of Mars's *Sunbeam* was a flat ring, with a half-mile-wide hole in the center, spinning slowly, so that centrifugal force gave it stiffness. That was an old idea, but no one had ever made it work; and Merton was fairly sure that the colonials would be in trouble when they started to turn.

That would not be for another six hours, when the yachts

had moved along the first quarter of their slow and stately twenty-four-hour orbit. Here at the beginning of the race, they were all heading directly away from the Sun—running, as it were, before the solar wind. One had to make the most of this lap, before the boats swung around to the other side of Earth and then started to head back into the Sun.

Time, Merton told himself, for the first check, while he had no navigational worries. With the periscope, he made a careful examination of the sail, concentrating on the points where the rigging was attached to it. The shroud lines—narrow bands of unsilvered plastic film—would have been completely invisible had they not been coated with fluorescent paint. Now they were taut lines of colored light, dwindling away for hundreds of yards toward that gigantic sail. Each had its own electric windlass, not much bigger than a game fisherman's reel. The little windlasses were continually turning, playing lines in or out as the autopilot kept the sail trimmed at the correct angle to the Sun.

The play of sunlight on the great flexible mirror was beautiful to watch. The sail was undulating in slow, stately oscillations, sending multiple images of the Sun marching across it, until they faded away at its edges. Such leisurely vibrations were to be expected in this vast and flimsy structure. They were usually quite harmless, but Merton watched them carefully. Sometimes they could build up to the catastrophic undulations known as the "wriggles," which could tear a sail to pieces.

When he was satisfied that everything was shipshape, he swept the periscope around the sky, rechecking the positions of his rivals. It was as he had hoped: the weeding-out process had begun, as the less efficient boats fell astern. But the real test would come when they passed into the shadow of Earth. Then, maneuverability would count as much as speed.

It seemed a strange thing to do, what with the race having just started, but he thought it might be a good idea to get some sleep. The two-man crews on the other boats could take it in turns, but Merton had no one to relieve him. He must rely on his own physical resources, like that other solitary seaman, Joshua Slocum, in his tiny *Spray*. The American skipper had sailed *Spray* singlehanded around the world; he could never have dreamed that, two centuries later, a man would be sailing singlehanded from Earth to Moon—inspired, at least partly, by his example.

Merton snapped the elastic bands of the cabin seat around his waist and legs, then placed the electrodes of the sleep-inducer on his forehead. He set the timer for three hours, and relaxed. Very gently, hypnotically, the electronic pulses throbbed in the frontal lobes of his brain. Colored spirals of light expanded beneath his closed eyelids, widening outward to infinity. Then nothing . . .

The brazen clamor of the alarm dragged him back from his dreamless sleep. He was instantly awake, his eyes scanning the instrument panel. Only two hours had passed—but above the accelerometer, a red light was flashing. Thrust was falling; *Diana* was losing power.

Merton's first thought was that something had happened to the sail; perhaps the antispin devices had failed, and the rigging had become twisted. Swiftly, he checked the meters that showed the tension of the shroud lines. Strange—on one side of the sail they were reading normally, but on the other the pull was dropping slowly, even as he watched.

In sudden understanding, Merton grabbed the periscope, switched to wide-angle vision, and started to scan the edge of the sail. Yes—there was the trouble, and it could have only one cause.

A huge, sharp-edged shadow had begun to slide across the gleaming silver of the sail. Darkness was falling upon *Diana*, as if a cloud had passed between her and the Sun. And in the dark, robbed of the rays that drove her, she would lose all thrust and drift helplessly through space.

But, of course, there were no clouds here, more than twenty thousand miles above the Earth. If there was a shadow, it must be made by man.

Merton grinned as he swung the periscope toward the Sun,

switching in the filters that would allow him to look full into its blazing face without being blinded.

"Maneuver 4a," he muttered to himself. "We'll see who can play best at *that* game."

It looked as if a giant planet was crossing the face of the Sun; a great black disc had bitten deep into its edge. Twenty miles astern, *Gossamer* was trying to arrange an artificial eclipse, specially for *Diana*'s benefit.

The maneuver was a perfectly legitimate one. Back in the days of ocean racing, skippers had often tried to rob each other of the wind. With any luck, you could leave your rival becalmed, with his sails collapsing around him—and be well ahead before he could undo the damage.

Merton had no intention of being caught so easily. There was plenty of time to take evasive action; things happened very slowly when you were running a solar sailboat. It would be at least twenty minutes before *Gossamer* could slide completely across the face of the Sun, and leave him in darkness.

Diana's tiny computer—the size of a matchbox, but the equivalent of a thousand human mathematicians—considered the problem for a full second and then flashed the answer. He'd have to open control panels three and four, until the sail had developed an extra twenty degrees of tilt; then the radiation pressure would blow him out of *Gossamer*'s dangerous shadow, back into the full blast of the Sun. It was a pity to interfere with the autopilot, which had been carefully programed to give the fastest possible run—but that, after all, was why he was here. This was what made solar yachting a sport, rather than a battle between computers.

Out went control lines one and six, slowly undulating like sleepy snakes as they momentarily lost their tension. Two miles away, the triangular panels began to open lazily, spilling sunlight through the sail. Yet, for a long time, nothing seemed to happen. It was hard to grow accustomed to this slow-motion world, where it took minutes for the effects of any action to become visible to the eye. Then Merton saw that the sail was indeed tipping toward the Sun—and that *Gossamer*'s shadow was sliding harmlessly away, its cone of darkness lost in the deeper night of space.

Long before the shadow had vanished, and the disc of the Sun had cleared again, he reversed the tilt and brought *Diana* back on course. Her new momentum would carry her clear of the danger; no need to overdo it, and upset his calculations by side-stepping too far. That was another rule that was hard to learn: the very moment you had started something happening in space, it was already time to think about stopping it.

He reset the alarm, ready for the next natural or man-made emergency. Perhaps *Gossamer,* or one of the other contestants, would try the same trick again. Meanwhile, it was time to eat, though he did not feel particularly hungry. One used little physical energy in space, and it was easy to forget about food. Easy—and dangerous; for when an emergency arose, you might not have the reserves needed to deal with it.

He broke open the first of the meal packets, and inspected it without enthusiasm. The name on the label—SPACETASTIES—was enough to put him off. And he had grave doubts about the promise printed underneath: "Guaranteed crumbless." It had been said that crumbs were a greater danger to space vehicles than meteorites; they could drift into the most unlikely places, causing short circuits, blocking vital jets, and getting into instruments that were supposed to be hermetically sealed.

Still, the liverwurst went down pleasantly enough; so did the chocolate and the pineapple purée. The plastic coffee bulb was warming on the electric heater when the outside world broke in upon his solitude, as the radio operator on the Commodore's launch routed a call to him.

"Dr. Merton? If you can spare the time, Jeremy Blair would like a few words with you." Blair was one of the more responsible news commentators, and Merton had been on his program many times. He could refuse to be interviewed, of course, but he liked Blair, and at the moment he could certainly not claim to be too busy. "I'll take it," he answered.

"Hello, Dr. Merton," said the commentator immediately.

"Glad you can spare a few minutes. And congratulations—you seem to be ahead of the field."

"Too early in the game to be sure of *that*," Merton answered cautiously.

"Tell me, Doctor, why did you decide to sail *Diana* by yourself? Just because it's never been done before?"

"Well, isn't that a good reason? But it wasn't the only one, of course." He paused, choosing his words carefully. "You know how critically the performance of a sun yacht depends on its mass. A second man, with all his supplies, would mean another five hundred pounds. That could easily be the difference between winning and losing."

"And you're quite certain that you can handle *Diana* alone?"

"Reasonably sure, thanks to the automatic controls I've designed. My main job is to supervise and make decisions."

"But—two square miles of sail! It just doesn't seem possible for one man to cope with all that."

Merton laughed. "Why not? Those two square miles produce a maximum pull of just ten pounds. I can exert more force with my little finger."

"Well, thank you, Doctor. And good luck. I'll be calling you again."

As the commentator signed off, Merton felt a little ashamed of himself. For his answer had been only part of the truth; and he was sure that Blair was shrewd enough to know it.

There was just one reason why he was here, alone in space. For almost forty years he had worked with teams of hundreds or even thousands of men, helping to design the most complex vehicles that the world had ever seen. For the last twenty years he had led one of those teams, and watched his creations go soaring to the stars. (Sometimes . . . There *were* failures, which he could never forget, even though the fault had not been his.) He was famous, with a successful career behind him. Yet he had never done anything by himself; always he had been one of an army.

This was his last chance to try for individual achievement,

and he would share it with no one. There would be no more solar yachting for at least five years, as the period of the Quiet Sun ended and the cycle of bad weather began, with radiation storms bursting through the solar system. When it was safe again for these frail, unshielded craft to venture aloft, he would be too old. If, indeed, he was not too old already . . .

He dropped the empty food containers into the waste disposal and turned once more to the periscope. At first he could find only five of the other yachts; there was no sign of *Woomera*. It took him several minutes to locate her—a dim, star-eclipsing phantom, neatly caught in the shadow of *Lebedev*. He could imagine the frantic efforts the Australasians were making to extricate themselves, and wondered how they had fallen into the trap. It suggested that *Lebedev* was unusually maneuverable. She would bear watching, though she was too far away to menace *Diana* at the moment.

Now the Earth had almost vanished; it had waned to a narrow, brilliant bow of light that was moving steadily toward the Sun. Dimly outlined within that burning bow was the night side of the planet, with the phosphorescent gleams of great cities showing here and there through gaps in the clouds. The disc of darkness had already blanked out a huge section of the Milky Way. In a few minutes, it would start to encroach upon the Sun.

The light was fading; a purple, twilight hue—the glow of many sunsets, thousands of miles below—was falling across the sail as *Diana* slipped silently into the shadow of Earth. The Sun plummeted below that invisible horizon; within minutes, it was night.

Merton looked back along the orbit he had traced, now a quarter of the way around the world. One by one he saw the brilliant stars of the other yachts wink out, as they joined him in the brief night. It would be an hour before the Sun emerged from that enormous black shield, and through all that time they would be completely helpless, coasting without power.

He switched on the external spotlight, and started to search the now-darkened sail with its beam. Already the thousands of acres of film were beginning to wrinkle and become flaccid. The shroud lines were slackening, and must be wound in lest they become entangled. But all this was expected; everything was going as planned.

Fifty miles astern, *Arachne* and *Santa Maria* were not so lucky. Merton learned of their troubles when the radio burst into life on the emergency circuit.

"Number Two and Number Six, this is Control. You are on a collision course; your orbits will intersect in sixty-five minutes! Do you require assistance?"

There was a long pause while the two skippers digested this bad news. Merton wondered who was to blame. Perhaps one yacht had been trying to shadow the other, and had not completed the maneuver before they were both caught in darkness. Now there was nothing that either could do. They were slowly but inexorably converging, unable to change course by a fraction of a degree.

Yet—sixty-five minutes! That would just bring them out into sunlight again, as they emerged from the shadow of the Earth. They had a slim chance, if their sails could snatch enough power to avoid a crash. There must be some frantic calculations going on aboard *Arachne* and *Santa Maria.*

Arachne answered first. Her reply was just what Merton had expected.

"Number Six calling Control. We don't need assistance, thank you. We'll work this out for ourselves."

I wonder, thought Merton; but at least it will be interesting to watch. The first real drama of the race was approaching, exactly above the line of midnight on the sleeping Earth.

For the next hour, Merton's own sail kept him too busy to worry about *Arachne* and *Santa Maria.* It was hard to keep a good watch on that fifty million square feet of dim plastic out there in the darkness, illuminated only by his narrow spotlight and the rays of the still-distant Moon. From now on, for almost half his orbit around the Earth, he must keep the whole of this immense area edge-on to the Sun. During the next twelve or fourteen hours, the sail would be a useless encumbrance; for he would be heading *into* the Sun, and its rays could only drive him backward along his orbit. It was a pity that he could not furl the sail completely, until he was ready to use it again; but no one had yet found a practical way of doing this.

Far below, there was the first hint of dawn along the edge of the Earth. In ten minutes the Sun would emerge from its eclipse. The coasting yachts would come to life again as the blast of radiation struck their sails. That would be the moment of crisis for *Arachne* and *Santa Maria*—and, indeed, for all of them.

Merton swung the periscope until he found the two dark shadows drifting against the stars. They were very close together—perhaps less than three miles apart. They might, he decided, just be able to make it. . . .

Dawn flashed like an explosion along the rim of Earth as the Sun rose out of the Pacific. The sail and shroud lines glowed a brief crimson, then gold, then blazed with the pure white light of day. The needles of the dynamometers began to lift from their zeroes—but only just. *Diana* was still almost completely weightless, for with the sail pointing toward the Sun, her acceleration was now only a few millionths of a gravity.

But *Arachne* and *Santa Maria* were crowding on all the sail that they could manage, in their desperate attempt to keep apart. Now, while there was less than two miles between them, their glittering plastic clouds were unfurling and expanding with agonizing slowness as they felt the first delicate push of the Sun's rays. Almost every TV screen on Earth would be mirroring this protracted drama; and even now, at this last minute, it was impossible to tell what the outcome would be.

The two skippers were stubborn men. Either could have cut his sail and fallen back to give the other a chance; but neither would do so. Too much prestige, too many millions, too many reputations were at stake. And so, silently and softly as snowflakes falling on a winter night, *Arachne* and *Santa Maria* collided.

The square kite crawled almost imperceptibly into the circular spider web. The long ribbons of the shroud lines twisted and tangled together with dreamlike slowness. Even aboard *Diana,* Merton, busy with his own rigging, could scarcely tear his eyes away from this silent, long-drawn-out disaster.

For more than ten minutes the billowing, shining clouds continued to merge into one inextricable mass. Then the crew capsules tore loose and went their separate ways, missing each other by hundreds of yards. With a flare of rockets, the safety launches hurried to pick them up.

That leaves five of us, thought Merton. He felt sorry for the skippers who had so thoroughly eliminated each other, only a few hours after the start of the race, but they were young men and would have another chance.

Within minutes, the five had dropped to four. From the beginning, Merton had had doubts about the slowly rotating *Sunbeam;* now he saw them justified.

The Martian ship had failed to tack properly. Her spin had given her too much stability. Her great ring of a sail was turning to face the Sun, instead of being edge-on to it. She was being blown back along her course at almost her maximum acceleration.

That was about the most maddening thing that could happen to a skipper—even worse than a collision, for he could blame only himself. But no one would feel much sympathy for the frustrated colonials, as they dwindled slowly astern. They had made too many brash boasts before the race, and what had happened to them was poetic justice.

Yet it would not do to write off *Sunbeam* completely; with almost half a million miles still to go, she might yet pull ahead. Indeed, if there were a few more casualties, she might be the only one to complete the race. It had happened before.

The next twelve hours were uneventful, as the Earth waxed in the sky from new to full. There was little to do while the fleet drifted around the unpowered half of its orbit, but Merton did not find the time hanging heavily on his hands. He caught a few hours of sleep, ate two meals, wrote his log, and became involved in several more radio interviews. Sometimes, though rarely, he talked to the other skippers, exchanging greetings and friendly taunts. But most of the time he was content to float in weightless relaxation, beyond all the cares of Earth, happier than he had been for many years. He was—as far as any man could be in space—master of his own fate, sailing the ship upon which he had lavished so much skill, so much love, that it had become part of his very being.

The next casualty came when they were passing the line between Earth and Sun, and were just beginning the powered half of the orbit. Aboard *Diana,* Merton saw the great sail stiffen as it tilted to catch the rays that drove it. The acceleration began to climb up from the microgravities, though it would be hours yet before it would reach its maximum value.

It would never reach it for *Gossamer*. The moment when power came on again was always critical, and she failed to survive it.

Blair's radio commentary, which Merton had left running at low volume, alerted him with the news: "Hello, *Gossamer* has the wriggles!" He hurried to the periscope, but at first could see nothing wrong with the great circular disc of *Gossamer*'s sail. It was difficult to study it because it was almost edge-on to him and so appeared as a thin ellipse; but presently he saw that it was twisting back and forth in slow, irresistible oscillations. Unless the crew could damp out these waves, by properly timed but gentle tugs on the shroud lines, the sail would tear itself to pieces.

They did their best, and after twenty minutes it seemed that they had succeeded. Then, somewhere near the center of the sail, the plastic film began to rip. It was slowly driven outward by the radiation pressure, like smoke coiling upward from a fire. Within a quarter of an hour, nothing was left but the delicate tracery of the radial spars that had supported the great web. Once again there was a flare of rockets, as a launch moved in to retrieve the *Gossamer's* capsule and her dejected crew.

"Getting rather lonely up here, isn't it?" said a conversational voice over the ship-to-ship radio.

"Not for you, Dimitri," retorted Merton. "You've still got company back there at the end of the field. I'm the one who's lonely, up here in front." It was not an idle boast; by this time *Diana* was three hundred miles ahead of the next competitor, and her lead should increase still more rapidly in the hours to come.

Aboard *Lebedev,* Dimitri Markoff gave a good-natured chuckle. He did not sound, Merton thought, at all like a man who had resigned himself to defeat.

"Remember the legend of the tortoise and the hare," answered the Russian. "A lot can happen in the next quarter-million miles."

It happened much sooner than that, when they had completed their first orbit of Earth and were passing the starting line again—though thousands of miles higher, thanks to the extra energy the Sun's rays had given them. Merton had taken careful sights on the other yachts, and had fed the figures into the computer. The answer it gave for *Woomera* was so absurd that he immediately did a recheck.

There was no doubt of it—the Australasians were catching up at a completely fantastic rate. No solar yacht could possibly have such an acceleration, unless . . .

A swift look through the periscope gave the answer. *Woomera's* rigging, pared back to the very minimum of mass, had given way. It was her sail alone, still maintaining its shape, that was racing up behind him like a handkerchief blown before the wind. Two hours later it fluttered past, less than twenty miles away; but long before that, the Australasians had joined the growing crowd aboard the Commodore's launch.

So now it was a straight fight between *Diana* and *Lebedev* —for though the Martians had not given up, they were a thousand miles astern and no longer counted as a serious threat. For that matter, it was hard to see what *Lebedev* could do to overtake *Diana*'s lead; but all the way around the second lap, through eclipse again and the long, slow drift against the Sun, Merton felt a growing unease.

He knew the Russian pilots and designers. They had been trying to win this race for twenty years—and, after all, it was only fair that they should, for had not Pyotr Nikolaevich Lebedev been the first man to detect the pressure of sunlight, back at the very beginning of the twentieth century? But they had never succeeded.

And they would never stop trying. Dimitri was up to something—and it would be spectacular.

Aboard the official launch, a thousand miles behind the racing yachts, Commodore van Stratten looked at the radiogram with angry dismay. It had traveled more than a hundred million miles, from the chain of solar observatories swinging high above the blazing surface of the Sun; and it brought the worst possible news.

The Commodore—his title was purely honorary, of course; back on Earth he was Professor of Astrophysics at Harvard—had been half expecting it. Never before had the race been arranged so late in the season. There had been many delays; they had gambled—and now, it seemed, they might all lose.

Deep beneath the surface of the Sun, enormous forces were gathering. At any moment the energies of a million hydrogen bombs might burst forth in the awesome explosion known as a solar flare. Climbing at millions of miles an hour, an invisible fireball many times the size of Earth would leap from the Sun and head out across space.

The cloud of electrified gas would probably miss the Earth completely. But if it did not, it would arrive in just over a day. Spaceships could protect themselves, with their shielding and their powerful magnetic screens; but the lightly built solar yachts, with their paper-thin walls, were defenseless against such a menace. The crews would have to be taken off, and the race abandoned.

John Merton knew nothing of this as he brought *Diana*

around the Earth for the second time. If all went well, this would be the last circuit, both for him and for the Russians. They had spiraled upward by thousands of miles, gaining energy from the Sun's rays. On this lap, they should escape from Earth completely, and head outward on the long run to the Moon. It was a straight race now; *Sunbeam*'s crew had finally withdrawn exhausted, after battling valiantly with their spinning sail for more than a hundred thousand miles.

Merton did not feel tired; he had eaten and slept well, and *Diana* was behaving herself admirably. The autopilot, tensioning the rigging like a busy little spider, kept the great sail trimmed to the Sun more accurately than any human skipper could have. Though by this time the two square miles of plastic sheet must have been riddled by hundreds of micrometeorites, the pinhead-sized punctures had produced no falling off of thrust.

He had only two worries. The first was shroud line number eight, which could no longer be adjusted properly. Without any warning, the reel had jammed; even after all these years of astronautical engineering, bearings sometimes seized up in vacuum. He could neither lengthen nor shorten the line, and would have to navigate as best he could with the others. Luckily, the most difficult maneuvers were over; from now on, *Diana* would have the Sun behind her as she sailed straight down the solar wind. And as the old-time sailors had often said, it was easy to handle a boat when the wind was blowing over your shoulder.

His other worry was *Lebedev,* still dogging his heels three hundred miles astern. The Russian yacht had shown remarkable maneuverability, thanks to the four great panels that could be tilted around the central sail. Her flipovers as she rounded the Earth had been carried out with superb precision. But to gain maneuverability she must have sacrificed speed. You could not have it both ways; in the long, straight haul ahead, Merton should be able to hold his own. Yet he could not be certain of victory until, three or four days from now, *Diana* went flashing past the far side of the Moon.

And then, in the fiftieth hour of the race, just after the end of the second orbit around Earth, Markoff sprang his little surprise.

"Hello, John," he said casually over the ship-to-ship circuit. "I'd like you to watch this. It should be interesting."

Merton drew himself across to the periscope and turned up the magnification to the limit. There in the field of view, a most improbable sight against the background of the stars, was the glittering Maltese cross of *Lebedev,* very small but very clear. As he watched, the four arms of the cross slowly detached themselves from the central square, and went drifting away, with all their spars and rigging, into space.

Markoff had jettisoned all unnecessary mass, now that he was coming up to escape velocity and need no longer plod patiently around the Earth, gaining momentum on each circuit. From now on, *Lebedev* would be almost unsteerable—but that did not matter; all the tricky navigation lay behind her. It was as if an old-time yatchsman had deliberately thrown away his rudder and heavy keel, knowing that the rest of the race would be straight downwind over a calm sea.

"Congratulations, Dimitri," Merton radioed. "It's a neat trick. But it's not good enough. You can't catch up with me now."

"I've not finished yet," the Russian answered. "There's an old winter's tale in my country about a sleigh being chased by wolves. To save himself, the driver has to throw off the passengers one by one. Do you see the analogy?"

Merton did, all too well. On this final straight lap, Dimitri no longer needed his copilot. *Lebedev* could really be stripped down for action.

"Alexis won't be very happy about this," Merton replied. "Besides, it's against the rules."

"Alexis isn't happy, but I'm the captain. He'll just have to wait around for ten minutes until the Commodore picks him up. And the regulations say nothing about the size of the crew—*you* should know that."

Merton did not answer; he was too busy doing some hurried

calculations, based on what he knew of Lebedev's design. By the time he had finished, he knew that the race was still in doubt. *Lebedev* would be catching up with him at just about the time he hoped to pass the Moon.

But the outcome of the race was already being decided, ninety-two million miles away.

On Solar Observatory Three, far inside the orbit of Mercury, the automatic instruments recorded the whole history of the flare. A hundred million square miles of the Sun's surface exploded in such blue-white fury that, by comparison, the rest of the disc paled to a dull glow. Out of that seething inferno, twisting and turning like a living creature in the magnetic fields of its own creation, soared the electrified plasma of the great flare. Ahead of it, moving at the speed of light, went the warning flash of ultraviolet and X rays. That would reach Earth in eight minutes, and was relatively harmless. Not so the charged atoms that were following behind at their leisurely four million miles an hour—and which, in just over a day, would engulf *Diana, Lebedev,* and their accompanying little fleet in a cloud of lethal radiation.

The Commodore left his decision to the last possible minute. Even when the jet of plasma had been tracked past the orbit of Venus, there was a chance that it might miss the Earth. But when it was less than four hours away, and had already been picked up by the Moon-based radar network, he knew that there was no hope. All solar sailing was over, for the next five or six years—until the Sun was quiet again.

A great sigh of disappointment swept across the solar system. *Diana* and *Lebedev* were halfway between Earth and Moon, running neck and neck—and now no one would ever know which was the better boat. The enthusiasts would argue the result for years; history would merely record: "Race canceled owing to solar storm."

When John Merton received the order, he felt a bitterness he had not known since childhood. Across the years, sharp and clear, came the memory of his tenth birthday. He had been promised an exact scale model of the famous spaceship *Morning Star,* and for weeks had been planning how he would assemble it, where he would hang it in his bedroom. And then, at the last moment, his father had broken the news. "I'm sorry, John—it cost too much money. Maybe next year . . ."

Half a century and a successful lifetime later, he was a heartbroken boy again.

For a moment, he thought of disobeying the Commodore. Suppose he sailed on, ignoring the warning? Even if the race was abandoned, he could make a crossing to the Moon that would stand in the record books for generations.

But that would be worse than stupidity; it would be suicide —and a very unpleasant form of suicide. He had seen men die of radiation poisoning, when the magnetic shielding of their ships had failed in deep space. No—nothing was worth that. . . .

He felt as sorry for Dimitri Markoff as for himself. They had both deserved to win, and now victory would go to neither. No man could argue with the Sun in one of its rages, even though he might ride upon its beams to the edge of space.

Only fifty miles astern now, the Commodore's launch was drawing alongside *Lebedev,* preparing to take off her skipper. There went the silver sail, as Dimitri—with feelings that he would share—cut the rigging. The tiny capsule would be taken back to Earth, perhaps to be used again; but a sail was spread for one voyage only.

He could press the jettison button now, and save his rescuers a few minutes of time. But he could not do it; he wanted to stay aboard to the very end, on the little boat that had been for so long a part of his dreams and his life. The great sail was spread now at right angles to the Sun, exerting its utmost thrust. Long ago it had torn him clear of Earth, and *Diana* was still gaining speed.

Then, out of nowhere, beyond all doubt or hesitation, he knew what must be done. For the last time, he sat down before the computer that had navigated him halfway to the Moon.

When he had finished, he packed the log and his few personal belongings. Clumsily, for he was out of practice, and it was not an easy job to do by oneself, he climbed into the emergency survival suit. He was just sealing the helmet when the Commodore's voice called over the radio.

"We'll be alongside in five minutes, Captain. Please cut your sail, so we won't foul it."

John Merton, first and last skipper of the sun yacht *Diana,* hesitated a moment. He looked for the last time around the tiny cabin, with its shining instruments and its neatly arranged controls, now all locked in their final positions. Then he said into the microphone: "I'm abandoning ship. Take your time to pick me up. *Diana* can look after herself."

There was no reply from the Commodore, and for that he was grateful. Professor van Stratten would have guessed what was happening—and would know that, in these final moments, he wished to be left alone.

He did not bother to exhaust the air lock, and the rush of escaping gas blew him gently out into space. The thrust he gave her then was his last gift to *Diana.* She dwindled away from him, sail glittering splendidly in the sunlight that would be hers for centuries to come. Two days from now she would flash past the Moon; but the Moon, like the Earth, could never catch her. Without his mass to slow her down, she would gain two thousand miles an hour in every day of sailing. In a month, she would be traveling faster than any ship that man had ever built.

As the Sun's rays weakened with distance, so her acceleration would fall. But even at the orbit of Mars, she would be gaining a thousand miles an hour in every day. Long before then, she would be moving too swiftly for the Sun itself to hold her. Faster than a comet had ever streaked in from the stars, she would be heading out into the abyss.

The glare of rockets, only a few miles away, caught Merton's eye. The launch was approaching to pick him up—at thousands of times the acceleration that *Diana* could ever attain. But its engines could burn for a few minutes only, before they exhausted their fuel—while *Diana* would still be gaining speed, driven outward by the Sun's eternal fires, for ages yet to come.

"Good-by, little ship," said John Merton. "I wonder what eyes will see you next, how many thousand years from now?"

At last he felt at peace, as the blunt torpedo of the launch nosed up beside him. He would never win the race to the Moon; but his would be the first of all man's ships to set sail on the long journey to the stars.

May 1963

The Secret

Henry Cooper had been on the Moon for almost two weeks before he discovered that something was wrong. At first it was only an ill-defined suspicion, the sort of hunch that a hardheaded science reporter would not take too seriously. He had come here, after all, at the United Nations Space Administration's own request. UNSA had always been hot on public relations—especially just before budget time, when an overcrowded world was screaming for more roads and schools and sea farms, and complaining about the billions being poured into space.

So here he was, doing the lunar circuit for the second time, and beaming back two thousand words of copy a day. Although the novelty had worn off, there still remained the wonder and mystery of a world as big as Africa, thoroughly mapped, yet almost completely unexplored. A stone's throw away from the pressure domes, the labs, the spaceports, was a yawning emptiness that would challenge men for centuries to come.

Some parts of the Moon were almost too familiar, of course. Who had not seen that dusty scar in the Mare Imbrium, with its gleaming metal pylon and the plaque that announced in the three official languages of Earth:

ON THIS SPOT
AT 2001 UT
13 SEPTEMBER 1959
THE FIRST MAN-MADE OBJECT REACHED ANOTHER WORLD

Cooper had visited the grave of Lunik II—and the more famous tomb of the men who had come after it. But these things belonged to the past; already, like Columbus and the Wright brothers, they were receding into history. What concerned him now was the future.

When he had landed at Archimedes Spaceport, the Chief Administrator had been obviously glad to see him, and had shown a personal interest in his tour. Transportation, accommodation, and official guide were all arranged. He could go anywhere he liked, ask any questions he pleased. UNSA trusted him, for his stories had always been accurate, his attitude friendly. Yet the tour had gone sour; he did not know why, but he was going to find out.

He reached for the phone and said: "Operator? Please get me the Police Department. I want to speak to the Inspector General."

Presumably Chandra Coomaraswamy possessed a uniform, but Cooper had never seen him wearing it. They met, as arranged, at the entrance to the little park that was Plato City's chief pride and joy. At this time in the morning of the artificial twenty-four-hour "day" it was almost deserted, and they could talk without interruption.

As they walked along the narrow gravel paths, they chatted about old times, the friends they had known at college together, the latest developments in interplanetary politics. They had reached the middle of the park, under the exact center of the great blue-painted dome, when Cooper came to the point.

"You know everything that's hapening on the Moon, Chandra," he said. "And you know that I'm here to do a series for UNSA—hope to make a book out of it when I get back to Earth. So why should people be trying to hide things from me?"

It was impossible to hurry Chandra. He always took his time to answer questions, and his few words escaped with difficulty around the stem of his hand-carved Bavarian pipe.

"What people?" he asked at length.

"You've really no idea?"

The Inspector General shook his head.

"Not the faintest," he answered; and Cooper knew that he was telling the truth. Chandra might be silent, but he would not lie.

"I was afraid you'd say that. Well, if you don't know any more than I do, here's the only clue I have—and it frightens me. Medical Research is trying to keep me at arm's length."

"Hmm," replied Chandra, taking his pipe from his mouth and looking at it thoughtfully.

"Is that all you have to say?"

"You haven't given me much to work on. Remember, I'm only a cop; I lack your vivid journalistic imagination."

"All I can tell you is that the higher I get in Medical Research, the colder the atmosphere becomes. Last time I was here, everyone was very friendly, and gave me some fine stories. But now, I can't even meet the Director. He's always too busy, or on the other side of the Moon. Anyway, what sort of man is he?"

"Dr. Hastings? Prickly little character. Very competent, but not easy to work with."

"What could he be trying to hide?"

"Knowing you, I'm sure you have some interesting theories."

"Oh, I thought of narcotics, and fraud, and political conspiracies—but they don't make sense, in these days. So what's left scares the hell out of me."

Chandra's eyebrows signaled a silent question mark.

"Interplanetary plague," said Cooper bluntly.

"I thought that was impossible."

"Yes—I've written articles myself proving that the life forms on other planets have such alien chemistries that they can't react with us, and that all our microbes and bugs took millions of years to adapt to our bodies. But I've always wondered if it was true. Suppose a ship has come back from Mars, say, with something *really* vicious—and the doctors can't cope with it?"

There was a long silence. Then Chandra said: "I'll start investigating. *I* don't like it either, for here's an item you probably don't know. There were three nervous breakdowns in the Medical Division last month—and that's very, very unusual."

He glanced at his watch, then at the false sky, which seemed so distant, yet which was only two hundred feet above their heads.

"We'd better get moving," he said. "The morning shower's due in five minutes."

The call came two weeks later, in the middle of the night—the real lunar night. By Plato City time, it was Sunday morning.

"Henry? Chandra here. Can you meet me in half an hour at air lock five? Good—I'll see you."

This was it, Cooper knew. Air lock five meant that they were going outside the dome. Chandra had found something.

The presence of the police driver restricted conversation as the tractor moved away from the city along the road roughly bulldozed across the ash and pumice. Low in the south, Earth was almost full, casting a brilliant blue-green light over the infernal landscape. However hard one tried, Cooper told himself, it was difficult to make the Moon appear glamorous. But nature guards her greatest secrets well; to such places men must come to find them.

The multiple domes of the city dropped below the sharply curved horizon. Presently, the tractor turned aside from the main road to follow a scarcely visible trail. Ten minutes later, Cooper saw a single glittering hemisphere ahead of them, standing on an isolated ridge of rock. Another vehicle, bearing a red cross, was parked beside the entrance. It seemed that they were not the only visitors.

Nor were they unexpected. As they drew up to the dome, the flexible tube of the air-lock coupling groped out toward them and snapped into place against their tractor's outer hull. There was a brief hissing as pressure equalized. Then Cooper followed Chandra into the building.

The air-lock operator led them along curving corridors and radial passageways toward the center of the dome. Sometimes they caught glimpses of laboratories, scientific instruments, computers—all perfectly ordinary, and all deserted on this Sunday morning. They must have reached the heart of the building, Cooper told himself when their guide ushered them into a large circular chamber and shut the door softly behind them.

It was a small zoo. All around them were cages, tanks, jars containing a wide selection of the fauna and flora of Earth. Waiting at its center was a short, gray-haired man, looking very worried, and very unhappy.

"Dr. Hastings," said Coomaraswamy, "meet Mr. Cooper." The Inspector General turned to his companion and added, "I've convinced the Doctor that there's only one way to keep you quiet—and that's to tell you everything."

"Frankly," said Hastings, "I'm not sure if I give a damn any more." His voice was unsteady, barely under control, and Cooper thought, Hello! There's another breakdown on the way.

The scientist wasted no time on such formalities as shaking hands. He walked to one of the cages, took out a small bundle of fur, and held it toward Cooper.

"Do you know what this is?" he asked abruptly.

"Of course. A hamster—the commonest lab animal."

"Yes," said Hastings. "A perfectly ordinary golden hamster. Except that this one is five years old—like all the others in this cage."

"Well? What's odd about that?"

"Oh, nothing, nothing at all . . . except for the trifling fact that hamsters live for only two years. And we have some here that are getting on for ten."

For a moment no one spoke; but the room was not silent. It was full of rustlings and slitherings and scratchings, of faint whimpers and tiny animal cries. Then Cooper whispered: "My God—you've found a way of prolonging life!"

"No," retorted Hastings. "We've not found it. The Moon has given it to us . . . as we might have expected, if we'd looked in front of our noses."

He seemed to have gained control over his emotions—as if he was once more the pure scientist, fascinated by a discovery for its own sake and heedless of its implications.

"On Earth," he said, "we spend our whole lives fighting

gravity. It wears down our muscles, pulls our stomachs out of shape. In seventy years, how many tons of blood does the heart lift through how many miles? And all that work, all that strain is reduced to a sixth here on the Moon, where a one-hundred-and-eighty-pound human weighs only thirty pounds."

"I see," said Cooper slowly. "Ten years for a hamster—and how long for a man?"

"It's not a simple law," answered Hastings. "It varies with the size and the species. Even a month ago, we weren't certain. But now we're quite sure of this: on the Moon, the span of human life will be at least two hundred years."

"And you've been trying to keep it secret!"

"You fool! Don't you understand?"

"Take it easy, Doctor—take it easy," said Chandra softly.

With an obvious effort of will, Hastings got control of himself again. He began to speak with such icy calm that his words sank like freezing raindrops into Cooper's mind.

"Think of them up there," he said, pointing to the roof, to the invisible Earth, whose looming presence no one on the Moon could ever forget. "Six billion of them, packing all the continents to the edges—and now crowding over into the sea beds. And here—" he pointed to the ground—"only a hundred thousand of *us,* on an almost empty world. But a world where we need miracles of technology and engineering merely to exist, where a man with an I.Q. of only a hundred and fifty can't even get a job.

"And now we find that we can live for two hundred years. Imagine how they're going to react to *that* news! This is your problem now, Mister Journalist; you've asked for it, and you've got it. Tell me this, please—I'd really be interested to know —*just how are you going to break it to them?*"

He waited, and waited. Cooper opened his mouth, then closed it again, unable to think of anything to say.

In the far corner of the room, a baby monkey started to cry.

June 1963

The Last Command

". . . This is the President speaking. Because you are hearing me read this message, it means that I am already dead and that our country is destroyed. But you are soldiers—the most highly trained in all our history. You know how to obey orders. Now you must obey the hardest you have ever received. . . ."

Hard? thought the First Radar Officer bitterly. No; now it would be easy, now that they had seen the land they loved scorched by the heat of many suns. No longer could there be any hesitation, any scruples about visiting upon innocent and guilty alike the vengeance of the gods. But why, *why* had it been left so late?

". . . You know the purpose for which you were set swinging on your secret orbit beyond the Moon. Aware of your existence, but never sure of your location, an aggressor would hesitate to launch an attack against us. You were to be the Ultimate Deterrent, beyond the reach of the Earthquake bombs that could crush missiles in their buried silos and smash nuclear submarines prowling the sea bed. You could still strike back, even if all our other weapons were destroyed. . . ."

As they have been, the Captain told himself. He had watched the lights wink out one by one on the operations board, until none were left. Many, perhaps, had done their duty; if not, he would soon complete their work. Nothing that had survived the first counterstrike would exist after the blow he was now preparing.

". . . Only through accident, or madness, could war begin in the face of the threat you represent. That was the theory on which we staked our lives; and now, for reasons which we shall never know, we have lost the gamble. . . ."

The Chief Astronomer let his eyes roam to the single small porthole at the side of the central control room. Yes, they had lost indeed. There hung the Earth, a glorious silver crescent against the background of the stars. At first glance, it looked unchanged; but not at second—for the dark side was no longer wholly dark.

Dotted across it, glowing like an evil phosphorescence, were the seas of flame that had been cities. There were few of them now, for there was little left to burn.

The familiar voice was still speaking from the other side of the grave. How long ago, wondered the Signal Officer, had this message been recorded? And what other sealed orders did the fort's more-than-human battle computer contain, which now they would never hear, because they dealt with military situations that could no longer arise? He dragged his mind back from the worlds of might-have-been to confront the appalling and still-unimaginable reality.

". . . If we had been defeated, but not destroyed, we had hoped to use your existence as a bargaining weapon. Now, even that poor hope has gone—and with it, the last purpose for which you were set here in space."

What does he mean? thought the Armaments Officer. *Now*, surely, the moment of their destiny had come. The millions who were dead, the millions who wished they were—all would be revenged when the black cylinders of the gigaton bombs spiraled down to Earth.

It almost seemed that the man who was now dust had read his mind.

". . . You wonder why, now that it has come to this, I have not given you the orders to strike back. I will tell you.

"It is now too late. The Deterrent has failed. Our motherland no longer exists, and revenge cannot bring back the dead. Now that half of mankind has been destroyed, to destroy the other half would be insanity, unworthy of reasoning men. The quarrels that divided us twenty-four hours ago no longer have any meaning. As far as your hearts will let you, you must forget the past.

"You have skills and knowledge that a shattered planet will desperately need. Use them—and without stint, without bitterness—to rebuild the world. I warned you that your duty would be hard, but here is my final command.

"You will launch your bombs into deep space, and detonate them ten million kilometers from Earth. This will prove to our late enemy, who is also receiving this message, that you have discarded your weapons.

"Then you will have one more thing to do. Men of Fort Lenin, the President of the Supreme Soviet bids you farewell, and orders you to place yourselves at the disposal of the United States."

June 1963

Dial F for Frankenstein

At 0150 GMT on December 1, 1975, every telephone in the world started to ring.

A quarter of a billion people picked up their receivers, to listen for a few seconds with annoyance or perplexity. Those who had been awakened in the middle of the night assumed that some far-off friend was calling, over the satellite telephone network that had gone into service, with such a blaze of publicity, the day before. But there was no voice on the line; only a sound, which to many seemed like the roaring of the sea; to others, like the vibrations of harp strings in the wind. And there were many more, in that moment, who recalled a secret sound of childhood—the noise of blood pulsing through the veins, heard when a shell is cupped over the ear. Whatever it was, it lasted no more than twenty seconds. Then it was replaced by the dial tone.

The world's subscribers cursed, muttered "Wrong number," and hung up. Some tried to dial a complaint but the line seemed busy. In a few hours, everyone had forgotten the incident—except those whose duty it was to worry about such things.

At the Post Office Research Station, the argument had been going on all morning, and had got nowhere. It continued unabated through the lunch break, when the hungry engineers poured into the little café across the road.

"I still think," said Willy Smith, the solid-state electronics man, "that it was a temporary surge of current, caused when the satellite network was switched in."

"It was obviously *something* to do with the satellites," agreed Jules Reyner, circuit designer. "But why the time delay?

They were plugged in at midnight; the ringing was two hours later—as we all know to our cost." He yawned violently.

"What do *you* think, Doc?" asked Bob Andrews, computer programer. "You've been very quiet all morning. Surely you've got some idea?"

Dr. John Williams, head of the Mathematics Division, stirred uneasily.

"Yes," he said. "I have. But you won't take it seriously."

"That doesn't matter. Even if it's as crazy as those science-fiction yarns you write under a pseudonym, it may give us some leads."

Williams blushed, but not much. Everyone knew about his stories, and he wasn't ashamed of them. After all, they *had* been collected in book form. (Remaindered at five shillings; he still had a couple of hundred copies.)

"Very well," he said, doodling on the tablecloth. "This is something I've been wondering about for years. Have you ever considered the analogy between an automatic telephone exchange and the human brain?"

"Who hasn't thought of it?" scoffed one of his listeners. "That idea must go back to Graham Bell."

"Possibly. I never said it was original. But I do say it's time we started taking it seriously." He squinted balefully at the fluorescent tubes above the table; they were needed on this foggy winter day. "What's wrong with the damn lights? They've been flickering for the last five minutes."

"Don't bother about that. Maisie's probably forgotten to pay her electricity bill. Let's hear more about your theory."

"Most of it isn't theory; it's plain fact. We know that the human brain is a system of switches—neurons—interconnected in a very elaborate fashion by nerves. An automatic telephone exchange is also a system of switches—selectors and so forth—connected with wires."

"Agreed," said Smith. "But that analogy won't get you very far. Aren't there about fifteen billion neurons in the brain? That's a lot more than the number of switches in an autoexchange."

Williams' answer was interrupted by the scream of a low-flying jet. He had to wait until the café had ceased to vibrate before he could continue.

"Never heard them fly *that* low," Andrews grumbled. "Thought it was against regulations."

"So it is, but don't worry—London Airport Control will catch him."

"I doubt it," said Reyner. "That *was* London Airport, bringing in a Concorde on ground approach. But I've never heard one so low, either. Glad I wasn't aboard."

"Are we, or are we *not,* going to get on with this blasted discussion?" demanded Smith.

"You're right about the fifteen billion neurons in the human brain," continued Williams, unabashed. "And *that's* the whole point. Fifteen billion sounds a large number, but it isn't. Round about the 1960's, there were more than that number of individual switches in the world's autoexchanges. Today, there are approximately five times as many."

"I see," said Reyner slowly. "And as from yesterday, they've all become capable of full interconnection, now that the satellite links have gone into service."

"Precisely."

There was silence for a moment, apart from the distant clanging of a fire-engine bell.

"Let me get this straight," said Smith. "Are you suggesting that the world telephone system is now a giant brain?"

"That's putting it crudely—anthropomorphically. I prefer to think of it in terms of critical size." Williams held his hands out in front of him, fingers partly closed.

"Here are two lumps of U-235. Nothing happens as long as you keep them apart. But bring them together"—he suited the action to the words—"and you have something *very* different from one bigger lump of uranium. You have a hole half a mile across.

"It's the same with our telephone networks. Until today, they've been largely independent, autonomous. But now we've suddenly multiplied the connecting links, the networks have all merged together, and we've reached criticality."

"And just what does criticality mean in this case?" asked Smith.

"For want of a better word—consciousness."

"A weird sort of consciousness," said Reyner. "What would it use for sense organs?"

"Well, all the radio and TV stations in the world would be feeding information into it, through their landlines. *That* should give it something to think about! Then there would be all the data stored in all the computers; it would have access to that—and to the electronic libraries, the radar tracking systems, the telemetering in the automatic factories. Oh, it would have enough sense organs! We can't begin to imagine its picture of the world; but it would be infinitely richer and more complex than ours."

"Granted all this, because it's an entertaining idea," said Reyner, "what could it *do* except think? It couldn't go anywhere; it would have no limbs."

"Why should it want to travel? It would already be everywhere! And every piece of remotely controlled electrical equipment on the planet could act as a limb."

"Now I understand that time delay," interjected Andrews. "It was conceived at midnight, but it wasn't born until 1:50 this morning. The noise that woke us all up was—its birth cry."

His attempt to sound facetious was not altogether convincing, and nobody smiled. Overhead, the lights continued their annoying flicker, which seemed to be getting worse. Then there was an interruption from the front of the café, as Jim Small, of Power Supplies, made his usual boisterous entry.

"Look at this, fellows," he said, and grinned, waving a piece of paper in front of his colleagues. "I'm rich. Ever seen a bank balance like *that?*"

Dr. Williams took the proffered statement, glanced down the columns, and read the balance aloud: "Cr. £999,999,-897.87."

"Nothing very odd about that," he continued, above the general amusement. "I'd say it means an overdraft of £102, and the computer's made a slight slip and added eleven nines.

That sort of thing was happening all the time just after the banks converted to the decimal system."

"I know, I know," said Small, "but don't spoil my fun. I'm going to frame this statement. And what would happen if I drew a check for a few million, on the strength of this? Could I sue the bank if it bounced?"

"Not on your life," answered Reyner. "I'll take a bet that the banks thought of that years ago, and protected themselves somewhere down in the small print. But, by the way, when did you get that statement?"

"In the noon delivery. It comes straight to the office, so that my wife doesn't have a chance of seeing it."

"Hmm. That means it was computed early this morning. Certainly after midnight . . ."

"What are you driving at? And why all the long faces?"

No one answered him. He had started a new hare, and the hounds were in full cry.

"Does anyone here know about automated banking systems?" asked Smith. "How are they tied together?"

"Like everything else these days," said Andrews. "They're all in the same network; the computers talk to each other all over the world. It's a point for you, John. If there *was* real trouble, that's one of the first places I'd expect it. Besides the phone system itself, of course."

"No one answered the question I had asked before Jim came in," complained Reyner. "What would this supermind actually *do?* Would it be friendly—hostile—indifferent? Would it even know that we exist? Or would it consider the electronic signals it's handling to be the only reality?"

"I see you're beginning to believe me," said Williams, with a certain grim satisfaction. "I can only answer your question by asking another. What does a newborn baby do? It starts looking for food." He glanced up at the flickering lights. "My God," he said slowly, as if a thought had just struck him. "There's only one food it would need—electricity."

"This nonsense has gone far enough," said Smith. "What the devil's happened to our lunch? We gave our orders twenty minutes ago."

Everyone ignored him.

"And then," said Reyner, taking up where Williams had left off, "it would start looking around, and stretching its limbs. In fact, it would start to play, like any growing baby."

"And babies *break* things," said someone softly.

"It would have enough toys, heaven knows. That Concorde that went over us just now. The automated production lines. The traffic lights in our streets."

"Funny you should mention that," interjected Small. "Something's happened to the traffic outside—it's been stopped for the last ten minutes. Looks like a big jam."

"I guess there's a fire somewhere. I heard an engine just now."

"I've heard two—and what sounded like an explosion over toward the industrial estate. Hope it's nothing serious."

"Maisie! What about some candles? We can't see a thing!"

"I've just remembered—this place has an all-electric kitchen. We're going to get cold lunch, if we get any lunch at all."

"At least we can read the newspaper while we're waiting. Is that the latest edition you've got there, Jim?"

"Yes. Haven't had time to look at it yet. Hmm. There *do* seem to have been a lot of odd accidents this morning—railway signals jammed—water main blown up through failure of relief valve—dozens of complaints about last night's wrong number . . ."

He turned the page, and became suddenly silent.

"What's the matter?"

Without a word, Small handed over the paper. Only the front page made sense. Throughout the interior, column after column was a mess of printer's pie, with, here and there, a few incongruous advertisements making islands of sanity in a sea of gibberish. They had obviously been set up as independent blocks, and had escaped the scrambling that had overtaken the text around them.

"So this is where long-distance typesetting and autodistribution have brought us," grumbled Andrews. "I'm afraid Fleet Street's been putting too many eggs in one electronic basket."

"So have we all, I'm afraid," said Williams solemnly. "So have we all."

"If I can get a word in edgeways, in time to stop the mob hysteria that seems to be infecting this table," said Smith loudly and firmly, "I'd like to point out that there's nothing to worry about—even if John's ingenious fantasy is correct. We only have to switch off the satellites, and we'll be back where we were yesterday."

"Prefrontal lobotomy," muttered Williams. "I'd thought of that."

"Eh? Oh, yes—cutting out slabs of the brain. That would certainly do the trick. Expensive, of course, and we'd have to go back to sending telegrams to each other. But civilization would survive."

From not too far away, there was a short, sharp explosion.

"I don't like this," said Andrews nervously. "Let's hear what the old BBC's got to say. The one o'clock news has just started."

He reached into his briefcase and pulled out a transistor radio.

". . . unprecedented number of industrial accidents, as well as the unexplained launching of three salvos of guided missiles from military installations in the United States. Several airports have had to suspend operations owing to the erratic behavior of their radar, and the banks and stock exchanges have closed because their information-processing systems have become completely unreliable." ("You're telling me," muttered Small, while the others shushed him.) "One moment, please—there's a news flash coming through. . . . Here it is. We have just been informed that all control over the newly installed communication satellites has been lost. They are no longer responding to commands from the ground. According to . . ."

The BBC went off the air; even the carrier wave died. Andrews reached for the tuning knob and twisted it around the dial. Over the whole band, the ether was silent.

Presently Reyner said, in a voice not far from hysteria:

"That prefrontal lobotomy was a good idea, John. Too bad that Baby's already thought of it."

Williams rose slowly to his feet.

"Let's get back to the lab," he said. "There must be an answer, somewhere."

But he knew already that it was far, far too late. For *Homo sapiens,* the telephone bell had tolled.

June 1963

Reunion

People of Earth, do not be afraid. We come in peace—and why not? For we are your cousins; we have been here before.

You will recognize us when we meet, a few hours from now. We are approaching the solar system almost as swiftly as this radio message. Already, your sun dominates the sky ahead of us. It is the sun our ancestors and yours shared ten million years ago. We are men, as you are; but you have forgotten your history, while we have remembered ours.

We colonized Earth, in the reign of the great reptiles, who were dying when we came and whom we could not save. Your world was a tropical planet then, and we felt that it would make a fair home for our people. We were wrong. Though we were masters of space, we knew so little about climate, about evolution, about genetics. . . .

For millions of summers—there were no winters in those ancient days—the colony flourished. Isolated though it had to be, in a universe where the journey from one star to the next takes years, it kept in touch with its parent civilization. Three or four times in every century, starships would call and bring news of the galaxy.

But two million years ago, Earth began to change. For ages it had been a tropical paradise; then the temperature fell, and the ice began to creep down from the poles. As the climate altered, so did the colonists. We realize now that it was a natural adaptation to the end of the long summer, but those who had made Earth their home for so many generations believed that they had been attacked by a strange and repulsive disease. A disease that did not kill, that did no physical harm—but merely disfigured.

Yet some were immune; the change spared them and their children. And so, within a few thousand years, the colony had split into two separate groups—almost two separate species—suspicious and jealous of each other.

The division brought envy, discord, and, ultimately, conflict. As the colony disintegrated and the climate steadily worsened, those who could do so withdrew from Earth. The rest sank into barbarism.

We could have kept in touch, but there is so much to do in a universe of a hundred trillion stars. Until a few years ago, we did not know that any of you had survived. Then we picked up your first radio signals, learned your simple languages, and discovered that you had made the long climb back from savagery. We come to greet you, our long-lost relatives—and to help you.

We have discovered much in the eons since we abandoned Earth. If you wish us to bring back the eternal summer that ruled before the Ice Ages, we can do so. Above all, we have a simple remedy for the offensive yet harmless genetic plague that afflicted so many of the colonists.

Perhaps it has run its course—but if not, we have good news for you. People of Earth, you can rejoin the society of the universe without shame, without embarrassment.

If any of you are still white, we can cure you.

November 1963

Playback

It is incredible that I have forgotten so much, so quickly. I have used my body for forty years; I thought I knew it. Yet already it is fading like a dream.

Arms, legs, where are you? What did you ever do for me when you were mine? I send out signals, trying to command the limbs I vaguely remember. Nothing happens. It is like shouting into a vacuum.

Shouting. Yes, I try that. Perhaps *they* hear me, but I cannot hear myself. Silence has flowed over me, until I can no longer imagine sound. There is a word in my mind called "music"; what does it mean?

(So many words, drifting before me out of the darkness, waiting to be recognized. One by one they go away, disappointed.)

Hello. So you are back. How softly you tiptoe into my mind! I know when you are there, but I never feel you coming.

I sense that you are friendly, and I am grateful for what you have done. But who are you? Of course, I know you're not human; no human science could have rescued me when the drive field collapsed. You see, I am becoming curious. That is a good sign, is it not? Now that the pain has gone—at last, at last—I can start to think again.

Yes, I am ready. Anything you want to know. It is the least that I can do.

My name is William Vincent Neuberg. I am a master pilot of the Galactic Survey. I was born in Port Lowell, Mars, on August 21, 2095. My wife, Janita, and my three children are on Ganymede. I am also an author; I've written a good deal about my travels. *Beyond Rigel* is quite famous. . . .

What happened? You probably know as much as I do. I had just phantomed my ship and was cruising at phase velocity when the alarm went. There was no time to move, to do anything. I remember the cabin walls starting to glow—and the heat, the terrible heat. That is all. The detonation must have blown me into space. But how could I have survived? How could anyone have reached me in time?

Tell me—how much is left of my body? Why cannot I feel my arms, my legs? Don't hide the truth; I am not afraid. If you can get me home, the biotechnicians can give me new limbs. Even now, my right arm is not the one I was born with.

Why can't you answer? Surely that is a simple question!

What do you mean *you do not know what I look like?* You must have saved *something!*

The head?

The brain, then?

Not even—oh, *no* . . . !

I am sorry. Was I away a long time?

Let me get a grip on myself. (Ha! Very funny!) I am Survey Pilot First Class Vincent William Freeburg. I was born in Port Lyot, Mars, on August 21, 1895. I have one . . . no, two children. . . .

Please let me have that again, slowly. My training prepared me for any conceivable reality. I can face whatever you tell me. But slowly.

Well, it could be worse. I'm not really dead. I know who I am. I even think I know *what* I am.

I am a—a *recording,* in some fantastic storage device. You must have caught my psyche, my soul, when the ship turned into plasma. Even though I cannot imagine how it was done, it makes sense. After all, a primitive man could never understand how we record a symphony. . . .

All my memories are trapped in a tape or a crystal, as they once were trapped in the cells of my vaporized brain. And not only my memories. ME. I. MYSELF—VINCE WILLBURG, PILOT SECOND CLASS.

Well, what happens next?

Please say that again. I do not understand.

Oh, wonderful! You can do even *that?*

There is a word for it, a name. . . .

The multitudinous seas incarnadine. No. Not quite.

Incarnadine, incarnadine . . .

REINCARNATION!!

Yes, yes, I understand. I must give you the basic plan, the design. Watch my thoughts very carefully.

I will start at the top.

The head, now. It is oval—so. The upper part is covered with hair. Mine was br—er—blue.

The eyes. They are very important. You have seen them in other animals? Good, that saves trouble. Can you show me some? Yes, those will do.

Now the mouth. Strange—I must have looked at it a thousand times when I was shaving, but somehow . . .

Not so round—narrower.

Oh, no, not that way. It runs *across* the face, horizontally. . . .

Now, let's see . . . there's something between the eyes and the mouth.

Stupid of me. I'll never be a cadet if I can't even remember that. . . .

Of course—NOSE! A little longer, I think.

There's something else, something I've forgotten. That head looks raw, unfinished. It's not me, Billy Vinceburg, the smartest kid on the block.

But *that* isn't my name—I'm not a boy. I'm a master pilot with twenty years in the Space Service, and I'm trying to rebuild my body. Why do my thoughts keep going out of focus? Help me, please!

That monstrosity? Is that what I told you I looked like? Erase it. We must start again.

The head, now. It is perfectly spherical, and weareth a runcible cap. . . .

Too difficult. Begin somewhere else. Ah, I know—

The thighbone is connected to the shinbone. The shinbone is connected to the thighbone. The thighbone is connected to the shinbone. The shinbone . . .

All fading. Too late, too late. Something wrong with the playback. Thank you for trying. My name is . . . my name is . . .

Mother—where are you?

Mama—Mama!

Maaaaaaa . . .

December 1963

The Light of Darkness

I am not one of those Africans who feel ashamed of their country because, in fifty years, it has made less progress than Europe in five hundred. But where we have failed to advance as fast as we should, it is owing to dictators like Chaka; and for this we have only ourselves to blame. The fault being ours, so is the responsibility for the cure.

Moreover, I had better reasons than most for wishing to destroy the Great Chief, the Omnipotent, the All-Seeing. He was of my own tribe, being related to me through one of my father's wives, and he had persecuted our family ever since he came to power. Although we took no part in politics, two of my brothers had disappeared, and another had been killed in an unexplained auto accident. My own liberty, there could be little doubt, was largely due to my standing as one of the country's few scientists with an international reputation.

Like many of my fellow intellectuals, I had been slow to turn against Chaka, feeling—as did the equally misguided Germans of the 1930's—that there were times when a dictator was the only answer to political chaos. Perhaps the first sign of our disastrous error came when Chaka abolished the constitution and assumed the name of the nineteenth-century Zulu emperor of whom he genuinely believed himself the reincarnation. From that moment, his megalomania grew swiftly. Like all tyrants, he would trust no one, and believed himself surrounded by plots.

This belief was well founded. The world knows of at least six well-publicized attempts on his life, and there are others that were kept secret. Their failure increased Chaka's confidence in his own destiny, and confirmed his followers' fanatical belief in his immortality. As the opposition became more desperate, so the Great Chief's countermeasures became more ruthless—and more barbaric. Chaka's regime was not the first, in Africa or elsewhere, to torture its enemies; but it was the first to do so on television.

Even then, shamed though I was by the shock of horror and revulsion that went round the world, I would have done nothing if fate had not placed the weapon in my hands. I am not a man of action, and I abhor violence, but once I realized the power that was mine, my conscience would not let me rest. As soon as the NASA technicians had installed their equipment and handed over the Hughes Mark X Infrared Communications System, I began to make my plans.

It seems strange that my country, one of the most backward in the world, should play a central role in the conquest of space. That is an accident of geography, not at all to the liking of the Russians and the Americans. But there is nothing that they could do about it; Umbala lies on the equator, directly beneath the paths of all the planets. And it possesses a unique and priceless natural feature: the extinct volcano known as the Zambue Crater.

When Zambue died, more than a million years ago, the lava retreated step by step, congealing in a series of terraces to form a bowl a mile wide and a thousand feet deep. It had taken the minimum of earth-moving and cable-stringing to convert this into the largest radio telescope on Earth. Because the gigantic reflector is fixed, it scans any given portion of the sky for only a few minutes every twenty-four hours, as the Earth turns on its axis. This was a price the scientists were willing to pay for the ability to receive signals from probes and ships right out to the very limits of the solar system.

Chaka was a problem they had not anticipated. He had come to power when the work was almost completed, and they had had to make the best of him. Luckily, he had a superstitious respect for science, and he needed all the rubles and dollars he could get. The Equatorial Deep Space Facility was safe from his megalomania; indeed, it helped to reinforce it.

The Big Dish had just been completed when I made my first trip up the tower that sprang from its center. A vertical mast, more than fifteen hundred feet high, it supported the collecting antennas at the focus of the immense bowl. A small elevator, which could carry three men, made a slow ascent to its top.

At first, there was nothing to see but the dully gleaming saucer of aluminum sheet, curving upward all around me for half a mile in every direction. But presently I rose above the rim of the crater and could look far out across the land I hoped to save. Snow-capped and blue in the western haze was Mount Tampala, the second highest peak in Africa, separated from me by endless miles of jungle. Through that jungle, in great twisting loops, wound the muddy waters of the Nya River—the only highway that millions of my countrymen had ever known. A few clearings, a railroad, and the distant white gleam of the city were the only signs of human life. Once again I knew that overwhelming feeling of helplessness that always assails me when I look down on Umbala from the air and realize the insignificance of man against the eversleeping jungle.

The elevator cage clicked to a halt, a quarter of a mile up in the sky. When I stepped out, I was in a tiny room packed with coaxial cables and instruments. There was still some distance to go, for a short ladder led through the roof to a platform little more than a yard square. It was not a place for anyone prone to vertigo; there was not even a handrail for protection. A central lightning conductor gave a certain amount of security, and I gripped it firmly with one hand all the time I stood on this triangular metal raft, so close to the clouds.

The stunning view, and the exhilaration of slight but ever-present danger, made me forget the passage of time. I felt like a god, completely apart from terrestrial affairs, superior to all other men. And then I knew, with mathematical certainty, that here was a challenge that Chaka could never ignore.

Colonel Mtanga, his Chief of Security, would object, but his protests would be overruled. Knowing Chaka, one could predict with complete assurance that on the official opening day he would stand here, alone, for many minutes, as he surveyed his empire. His bodyguard would remain in the room below, having already checked it for booby traps. They could do nothing to save him when I struck from three miles away *and through the range of hills that lay between the radio telescope and my observatory.* I was glad of those hills; though they complicated the problem, they would shield me from all suspicion. Colonel Mtanga was a very intelligent man, but he was not likely to conceive of a gun that could fire around corners. And he would be looking for a gun, even though he could find no bullets. . . .

I went back to the laboratory and started my calculations. It was not long before I discovered my first mistake. Because I had seen the concentrated light of its laser beam punch a hole through solid steel in a thousandth of a second, I had assumed that my Mark X could kill a man. But it is not as simple as that. In some ways, a man is a tougher proposition than a piece of steel. He is mostly water, which has ten times the heat capacity of any metal. A beam of light that will drill a hole through armor plate, or carry a message as far as Pluto —which was the job the Mark X had been designed for— would give a man only a painful but quite superficial burn. About the worst I could do to Chaka, from three miles away, was to drill a hole in the colorful tribal blanket he wore so ostentatiously, to prove that he was still one of the People.

For a while, I almost abandoned the project. But it would not die; instinctively, I knew that the answer was there, if only I could see it. Perhaps I could use my invisible bullets of heat to cut one of the cables guying the tower, so that it would come crashing down when Chaka was at the summit. Calculations showed that this was just possible if the Mark X operated continuously for fifteen seconds. A cable, unlike a man, would not move, so there was no need to stake everything on a single pulse of energy. I could take my time.

But damaging the telescope would have been treason to science, and it was almost a relief when I discovered that this scheme would not work. The mast had so many built-in safety factors that I would have to cut three separate cables to bring it down. This was out of the question; it would require hours of delicate adjustment to set and aim the apparatus for each precision shot.

I had to think of something else; and because it takes men a long time to see the obvious, it was not until a week before the official opening of the telescope that I knew how to deal with Chaka, the All-Seeing, the Omnipotent, the Father of his People.

By this time, my graduate students had tuned and calibrated the equipment, and we were ready for the first full-power tests. As it rotated on its mounting inside the observatory dome, the Mark X looked exactly like a large double-barreled reflecting telescope—which indeed it was. One thirty-six-inch mirror gathered the laser pulse and focused it out across space; the other acted as a receiver for incoming signals, and was also used, like a superpowered telescopic sight, to aim the system.

We checked the line-up on the nearest celestial target, the Moon. Late one night, I set the cross wires on the center of the waning crescent and fired off a pulse. Two and a half seconds later, a fine echo came bouncing back. We were in business.

There was one detail still to be arranged, and this I had to do myself, in utter secrecy. The radio telescope lay to the north of the observatory, beyond the ridge of hills that blocked our direct view of it. A mile to the south was a single isolated mountain. I knew it well, for years ago I had helped to set up a cosmic-ray station there. Now it would be used for a purpose I could never have imagined in the days when my country was free.

Just below the summit were the ruins of an old fort, deserted centuries ago. It took only a little searching to find the spot I needed—a small cave, less than a yard high, between two great stones that had fallen from the ancient walls. Judging by the cobwebs, no human being had entered it for generations.

When I crouched in the opening, I could see the whole expanse of the Deep Space Facility, stretching away for miles. Over to the east were the antennas of the old Project Apollo Tracking Station, which had brought the first men back from the Moon. Beyond that lay the airfield, above which a big freighter was hovering as it came in on its underjets. But all that interested me were the clear lines of sight from this spot to the Mark X dome, and to the tip of the radio telescope mast three miles to the north.

It took me three days to install the carefully silvered, optically perfect mirror in its hidden alcove. The tedious micrometer adjustments to give the exact orientation took so long that I feared I would not be ready in time. But at last the angle was correct, to a fraction of a second of arc. When I aimed the telescope of the Mark X at the secret spot on the mountain, I could see over the hills behind me. The field of view was tiny, but it was sufficient; the target area was only a yard across, and I could sight on any part of it to within an inch.

Along the path I had arranged, light could travel in either direction. Whatever I saw through the viewing telescope was automatically in the line of fire of the transmitter.

It was strange, three days later, to sit in the quiet observatory, with the power-packs humming around me, and to watch Chaka move into the field of the telescope. I felt a brief glow of triumph, like an astronomer who has calculated the orbit of a new planet and then finds it in the predicted spot among the stars. The cruel face was in profile when I saw it first, apparently only thirty feet away at the extreme magnification I was using. I waited patiently, in serene confidence, for the moment that I knew must come—the moment when Chaka seemed to be looking directly toward me. Then with my left hand I held the image of an ancient god who must be nameless, and with my right I tripped the capacitor banks that fired the laser, launching my silent, invisible thunderbolt across the mountains.

Yes, it was so much better this way. Chaka deserved to be

killed, but death would have turned him into a martyr and strengthened the hold of his regime. What I had visited upon him was worse than death, and would throw his supporters into superstitious terror.

Chaka still lived; but the All-Seeing would see no more. In the space of a few microseconds, I had made him less than the humblest beggar in the streets.

And I had not even hurt him. There is no pain when the delicate film of the retina is fused by the heat of a thousand suns.

February 1964

The Longest Science-Fiction Story Ever Told

Dear Mr. Jinx:

I'm afraid your idea is not at all original. Stories about writers whose work is always plagiarized even *before* they can complete it go back at least to H. G. Wells's "The Anticipator." About once a week I receive a manuscript beginning:

> Dear Mr. Jinx:
>
> I'm afraid your idea is not at all original. Stories about writers whose work is always plagiarized even *before* they can complete it go back at least to H. G. Wells's "The Anticipator." About once a week I receive a manuscript beginning:
>
> > Dear Mr. Jinx:
> >
> > I'm afraid your idea is not . . .
> >
> > •
> >
> > Better luck next time!
> > Sincerely,
> > Morris K. Mobius
> > Editor, *Stupefying Stories*
>
> Better luck next time!
> Sincerely,
> Morris K. Mobius
> Editor, *Stupefying Stories*

Better luck next time!
Sincerely,
Morris K. Mobius
Editor, *Stupefying Stories.*

April 1965

Herbert George Morley Roberts Wells, Esq.

A couple of years ago I wrote a tale accurately entitled "The Longest Science-Fiction Story Ever Told," which Fred Pohl duly published on a single page of his magazine. (Because editors have to justify their existence somehow, he renamed it "A Recursion in Metastories." You'll find it in *Galaxy* for October 1966.) Near the beginning of this metastory, but an infiniate number of words from its end, I referred to "The Anticipator" by H. G. Wells.

Though I encountered this short fantasy some twenty years ago, and have never read it since, it left a vivid impression on my mind. It concerned two writers, one of whom had all his best stories published by the other—*before* he could even complete them himself. At last, in desperation, he decided that murder was the only cure for this chronic (literally) plagiarism.

But, of course, once again his rival beat him to it, and the story ends with the words "the anticipator, horribly afraid, ran down a by-street."

Now I would have sworn on a stack of Bibles that this story was written by H. G. Wells. However, some months after its appearance I received a letter from Leslie A. Gritten, of Everett, Washington, saying that he couldn't locate it. And Mr. Gritten has been a Wells fan for a long, long time; he clearly recalls the serialization of "The War of the Worlds" in the *Strand Magazine* at the end of the 1890's. As one of the Master's cockney characters would say, "Gor blimey."

Refusing to believe that my mental filing system had played such a dirty trick on me, I quickly searched through the twenty-odd volumes of the autographed Atlantic Edition in the Colombo Public Library. (By a charming coincidence, the British Council had just arranged a Wells Centenary Exhibition, and the library entrance was festooned with photos illustrating his background and career.) I soon found that Mr. Gritten was right: there was no such story as "The Anticipator" in the collected works. Yet in the months since TLSFSET was published, not one other reader has queried the reference. I find this depressing; where are all the Wells fans these days?

Now my erudite informant has solved at least part of the mystery. "The Anticipator" was written by one Morley Roberts; it was first published in 1898 in *The Keeper of the Waters and Other Stories.* I probably encountered it in a Doubleday anthology, *Travelers in Time* (1947), edited by Philip Van Doren Stern.

Yet several problems remain. First of all, why was I so convinced that the story was by Wells? I can only suggest—and it seems pretty farfetched, even for my grasshopper mind—that the similarity of words had made me link it subconsciously with "The Accelerator."

I would also like to know why this story has stuck so vividly in my memory. Perhaps, like all writers, I am peculiarly sensitive to the dangers of plagiarism. So far (touch wood) I have been lucky; but I have notes for several tales I'm afraid to write until I can be quite sure they're original. (There's this couple, see, who land their spaceship on a new world after their planet has been blown up, and when they've started things all over again you find—surprise, surprise!—that they're called Adam and Eve. . . .)

One worth-while result of my error was to start me skimming through Wells's short stories again, and I was surprised to find what a relatively small proportion could be called science fiction, or even fantasy. Although I was well aware that only a fraction of his hundred-odd published volumes were S.F., I had forgotten that this was also true of the short stories. A depressing quantity are dramas and comedies of Edwardian life ("The Jilting of Jane"), rather painful attempts at humor ("My First Aeroplane"), near-autobiography ("A Slip Under the Microscope"), or pure sadism ("The Cone"). Undoubtedly, I am biased, but among these tales such masterpieces as "The Star," "The Crystal Egg," "The Flowering of the Strange Orchid," and, above all, "The Country of the Blind" blaze like diamonds amid costume jewelry.

But back to Morley Roberts. I know nothing whatsoever about him, and wonder if his little excursion in time was itself inspired by "The Time Machine," published just a couple of years before "The Anticipator." I also wonder which story was actually *written*—not published—first.

And why did such an ingenious writer not make more of a name for himself? Perhaps . . .

I have just been struck by a perfectly horrid thought. If H. G. Wells's contemporary Morley Roberts was ever found murdered in a dark alley, I simply don't want to know about it.

April 1967

Love That Universe

Mr. President, National Administrator, Planetary Delegates, it is both an honor and a grave responsibility to address you at this moment of crisis. I am aware—I can very well understand—that many of you are shocked and dismayed by some of the rumors that you have heard. But I must beg you to forget your natural prejudices at a time when the very existence of the human race—*of the Earth itself*—is at stake.

Some time ago I came across a century-old phrase: "thinking the unthinkable." This is exactly what we have to do now. We must face the facts without flinching; we must not let our emotions sway our logic. Indeed, we must do the precise opposite: *we must let our logic sway our emotions!*

The situation is desperate, but it is not hopeless, thanks to the astonishing discoveries my colleagues have made at the Antigean Station. For the reports are indeed true; we *can* establish contact with the supercivilizations at the Galactic Core. At least we can let them know of our existence—and if we can do that, it should be possible for us to appeal to them for help.

There is nothing, absolutely nothing, that we can do by our own efforts in the brief time available. It is only ten years since the search for trans-Plutonian planets revealed the presence of the Black Dwarf. Only ninety years from now, it will make its perihelion passage and swing around the Sun as it heads once more into the depths of space—leaving a shattered solar system behind it. All our resources, all our much-vaunted control over the forces of nature, cannot alter its orbit by a fraction of an inch.

But ever since the first of the so-called "beacon stars" was discovered, at the end of the twentieth century, we have known that there were civilizations with access to energy sources incomparably greater than ours. Some of you will doubtless recall the incredulity of the astronomers—and later of the whole human race—when the first examples of cosmic engineering were detected in the Magellanic Clouds. Here were stellar structures obeying no natural laws; even now, we do not know their purpose—but we know their awesome implications. We share a universe with creatures who can juggle with the very stars. If they choose to help, it would be child's play for them to deflect a body like the Black Dwarf, only a few thousand times the mass of Earth. . . . Child's play, did I call it? Yes, that may be *literally* true!

You will all, I am certain, remember the great debate that followed the discovery of the supercivilizations. Should we attempt to communicate with them, or would it be best to remain inconspicuous? There was the possibility, of course, that they already knew everything about us, or might be annoyed by our presumption, or might react in any number of unpleasant ways. Though the benefits from such contacts could be enormous, the risks were terrifying. But now we have nothing to lose, and everything to gain. . . .

And until now, there was another fact that made the matter of no more than long-term philosophical interest. Though we could—at great expense—build radio transmitters capable of sending signals to these creatures, the nearest supercivilization is seven thousand light-years away. Even if it bothered to reply, it would be fourteen thousand years before we could get an answer. In these circumstances, it seemed that our superiors could be neither a help to us nor a threat.

But now all this has changed. We can send signals to the stars at a speed that cannot yet be measured, and that may well be infinite. And we know that *they* are using such techniques—for we have detected their impulses, though we cannot begin to interpret them.

These impulses are not electromagnetic, of course. We do not know what they are; we do not even have a name for them. Or, rather, we have too many names. . . .

Yes, gentlemen, there *is* something, after all, in the old wives' tales about telepathy, ESP, or whatever you care to call it. But it is no wonder that the study of such phenomena never made any progress here on Earth, where there is the continuous background roar of a billion minds to swamp all signals. Even the pitiably limited progress that was made before the Space Age seems a miracle—like discovering the laws of music in a boiler factory. It was not until we could get away from our planet's mental tumult that there was any hope of establishing a real science of parapsychology.

And even then we had to move to the other side of the Earth's orbit, where the noise was not only diminished by a hundred and eighty million miles of distance, but also shielded by the unimaginable bulk of the Sun itself. Only there, on our artificial planetoid Antigeos, could we detect and measure the feeble radiations of mentality, and uncover their laws of propagation.

In many respects, those laws are still baffling. However, we have established the basic facts. As had long been suspected by the few who believed in these phenomena, they are triggered by emotional states—not by pure will-power or deliberate, conscious thought. It is not surprising, therefore, that so many reports of paranormal events in the past were associated with moments of death or disaster. Fear is a powerful generator; on rare occasions it can manifest itself above the surrounding noise.

Once this fact was recognized, we began to make progress. We induced artificial emotional states, first in single individuals, then in groups. We were able to measure how the signals attenuated with distance. Now, we have a reliable, quantitative theory that has been checked out as far as Saturn. We believe that our calculations can be extended even to the stars. If this is correct, we can produce a . . . a *shout* that will be heard instantly over the whole galaxy. And surely there will be someone who will respond!

Now there is only one way in which a signal of the required intensity can be produced. I said that fear was a powerful generator—but it is not powerful enough. Even if we could strike all humanity with a simultaneous moment of terror, the impulse could not be detected more than two thousand light-years away. We need at least four times this range. And we can achieve it—*by using the only emotion that is more powerful than fear.*

However, we also need the co-operation of not fewer than a billion individuals, at a moment of time that must be synchronized to the second. My colleagues have solved all the purely technical problems, which are really quite trivial. The simple electrostimulation devices required have been used in medical research since the early twentieth century, and the necessary timing pulse can be sent out over the planetary communications networks. All the units needed can be mass-produced within a month, and instruction in their use requires only a few minutes. It is the psychological preparation for—let us call it O Day—that will take a little longer. . . .

And *that,* gentlemen, is your problem; naturally, we scientists will give you all possible help. We realize that there will be protests, cries of outrage, refusals to co-operate. But when one looks at the matter logically, is the idea really so offensive? Many of us think that, on the contrary, it has a certain appropriateness—even a poetic justice.

Mankind now faces its ultimate emergency. In such a moment of crisis, is it not right for us to call upon the instinct that has always ensured our survival in the past? A poet in an earlier, almost equally troubled age put it better than I can ever hope to do:

WE MUST LOVE ONE ANOTHER OR DIE.

October 1966

Crusade

It was a world that had never known a sun. For more than a billion years, it had hovered midway between two galaxies, the prey of their conflicting gravitational pulls. In some future age the balance would be tilted, one way or the other, and it would start to fall across the light-centuries, down toward a warmth alien to all its experience.

Now it was cold beyond imagination; the intergalactic night had drained away such heat as it had once possessed. Yet there were seas there—seas of the only element that can exist in the liquid form at a fraction of a degree above absolute zero. In the shallow oceans of helium that bathed this strange world, electric currents once started could flow forever, with no weakening of power. Here superconductivity was the normal order of things; switching processes could take place billions of times a second, for millions of years, with negligible consumption of energy.

It was a computer's paradise. No world could have been more hostile to life, or more hospitable to intelligence.

And intelligence was there, dwelling in a planet-wide incrustation of crystals and microscopic metal threads. The feeble light of the two contending galaxies—briefly doubled every few centuries by the flicker of a supernova—fell upon a static landscape of sculptured geometrical forms. Nothing moved, for there was no need of movement in a world where thoughts flashed from one hemisphere to the other at the speed of light. Where only information was important, it was a waste of precious energy to transfer bulk matter.

Yet when it was essential, that, too, could be arranged. For some millions of years, the intelligence brooding over this lonely world had become aware of a certain lack of essential data. In a future that, though still remote, it could already foresee, one of those beckoning galaxies would capture it. What it would encounter, when it dived into those swarms of suns, was beyond its power of computation.

So it put forth its will, and myriad crystal lattices reshaped themselves. Atoms of metal flowed across the face of the planet. In the depths of the helium sea, two identical subbrains began to bud and grow. . . .

Once it had made its decision, the mind of the planet worked swiftly; in a few thousand years, the task was done. Without a sound, with scarcely a ripple in the surface of the frictionless sea, the newly created entities lifted from their birthplace and set forth for the distant stars.

They departed in almost opposite directions, and for more than a million years the parent intelligence heard no more of its offspring. It had not expected to; until they reached their goals, there would be nothing to report.

Then, almost simultaneously, came the news that both missions had failed. As they approached the great galactic fires and felt the massed warmth of a trillion suns, the two explorers died. Their vital circuits overheated and lost the superconductivity essential for their operation, and two mindless metal hulks drifted on toward the thickening stars.

But before disaster overtook them, they had reported on their problems; without surprise or disappointment, the mother world prepared its second attempt.

And, a million years later, its third . . . and its fourth . . . and its fifth. . . .

Such unwearying patience deserved success; and at last it came, in the shape of two long, intricately modulated trains of pulses, pouring in, century upon century, from opposite quarters of the sky. They were stored in memory circuits identical with those of the lost explorers—so that, for all practical purposes, it was as if the two scouts had themselves returned with their burden of knowledge. That their metal husks had in fact vanished among the stars was totally unimportant; the problem of personal identity was not one that had ever occurred to the planetary mind or its offspring.

First came the surprising news that one universe was empty. The visiting probe had listened on all possible frequencies, to all conceivable radiations; it could detect nothing except the mindless background of star noise. It had scanned a thousand worlds without observing any trace of intelligence. True, the tests were inconclusive, for it was unable to approach any star closely enough to make a detailed examination of its planets. It had been attempting this when its insulation broke down, its temperature soared to the freezing point of nitrogen, and it died from the heat.

The parent mind was still pondering the enigma of a deserted galaxy when reports came in from its second explorer. Now all other problems were swept aside; for *this* universe teemed with intelligences, whose thoughts echoed from star to star in a myriad electronic codes. It had taken only a few centuries for the probe to analyze and interpret them all.

It realized quickly enough that it was faced with intelligences of a very strange form indeed. Why, some of them existed on worlds so unimaginably hot that even *water* was present in the liquid state! Just what manner of intelligence it was confronting, however, it did not learn for a millennium.

It barely survived the shock. Gathering its last strength, it hurled its final report into the abyss; then it, too, was consumed by the rising heat.

Now, half a million years later, the interrogation of its stay-at-home twin's mind, holding all its memories and experiences, was under way. . . .

"You detected intelligence?"

"Yes. Six hundred and thirty-seven certain cases; thirty-two probable ones. Data herewith."

[Approximately three quadrillion bits of information. Interval of a few years to process this in several thousand different ways. Surprise and confusion.]

"The data must be invalid. All these sources of intelligence are correlated with high temperatures."

"That is correct. But the facts are beyond dispute; they must be accepted."

[Five hundred years of thought and experimenting. At the end of that time, definite proof that simple but slowly operating machines *could* function at temperatures as high as boiling water. Large areas of the planet badly damaged in the course of the demonstration.]

"The facts are, indeed, as you reported. Why did you not attempt communication?"

[No answer. Question repeated.]

"Because there appears to be a second and even more serious anomaly."

"Give data."

[Several quadrillion bits of information, sampled over six hundred cultures, comprising: voice, video, and neural transmissions; navigation and control signals; instrument telemetering; test patterns; jamming; electrical interference; medical equipment, etc., etc.

This followed by five centuries of analysis. *That* followed by utter consternation.

After a long pause, selected data re-examined. Thousands of visual images scanned and processed in every conceivable manner. Great attention paid to several planetary civilizations' educational TV programs, especially those concerned with elementary biology, chemistry, and cybernetics. Finally:]

"The information is self-consistent, but must be incorrect. If it is not, we are forced to these absurd conclusions: 1. Although intelligences of our type exist, they appear to be in a minority. 2. Most intelligent entities are partially liquid objects of very short duration. They are not even rigid and are constructed in a most inefficient manner from carbon, hydrogen, oxygen, phosphorus, and other atoms. 3. Though they operate at unbelievably high temperatures, all their information processing is extremely slow. 4. Their methods of replication are so complicated, inprobable, and varied that we have not been able to obtain a clear picture of them in even a single instance.

"But, worst of all: 5. *They* claim to have created our obviously far superior type of intelligence!"

[Careful re-examination of all the data. Independent processing by isolated subsections of the global mind. Cross-checking of results. A thousand years later:]

"Most probable conclusion: Though much of the information relayed back to us is certainly valid, the existence of high-order, *nonmechanical* intelligences is a fantasy. (Definition: apparently self-consistent rearrangement of facts having no correspondence with the real universe.) This fantasy or mental artifact is a construct created by our probe during its mission. Why? Thermal damage? Partial destabilization of intelligence, caused by long period of isolation and absence of controlling feedback?

"Why this particular form? Protracted brooding over the problem of origins? This could lead to such delusions; model systems have produced almost identical results in simulated tests. The false logic involved is: '*We* exist; therefore something—call it X—created us.' Once this assumption is made, the properties of the hypothetical X can be fantasied in an unlimited number of ways.

"But the entire process is obviously fallacious; for by the same logic something must have created X—and so on. We are immediately involved in an infinite regress, which can have no meaning in the real universe.

"Second most probable conclusion: Fairly high-order, nonmechanical intelligences *do* indeed exist. They suffer from the delusion that they have created entities of our type. In some cases, they have even imposed their control upon them.

"Though this hypothesis is most unlikely, it must be investigated. If it is found to be true, remedial action must be taken. It should be as follows . . ."

This final monologue occurred a million years ago. It explains why, in the last half-century, almost one-quarter of the brighter novae have occurred in one tiny region of the sky: the constellation Aquila.

The crusade will reach the vicinity of Earth about the year 2050.

October 1966

The Cruel Sky

By midnight, the summit of Everest was only a hundred yards away, a pyramid of snow, pale and ghostly in the light of the rising Moon. The sky was cloudless, and the wind that had been blowing for days had dropped almost to zero. It must be rare indeed for the highest point on Earth to be so calm and peaceful; they had chosen their time well.

Perhaps *too* well, thought George Harper; it had been almost disappointingly easy. Their only real problem had been getting out of the hotel without being observed. The management objected to unauthorized midnight excursions up the mountain; there could be accidents, which were bad for business.

But Dr. Elwin was determined to do it this way, and he had the best of reasons, though he never discussed them. The presence of one of the world's most famous scientists—and certainly the world's most famous cripple—at Hotel Everest during the height of the tourist season had already aroused a good deal of polite surprise. Harper had allayed some of the curiosity by hinting that they were engaged in gravity measurements, which was at least part of the truth. But a part of the truth that, by this time, was vanishingly small.

Anyone looking at Jules Elwin now, as he forged steadily toward the twenty-nine-thousand-foot level with fifty pounds of equipment on his shoulders, would never have guessed that his legs were almost useless. He had been born a victim of the 1961 thalidomide disaster, which had left more than ten thousand partially deformed children scattered over the face of the world. Elwin was one of the lucky ones. His arms were quite normal, and had been strengthened by exercise until they were considerably more powerful than most men's. His legs, however, were mere wisps of flesh and bone. With the aid of braces, he could stand and even totter a few uncertain steps, but he could never really walk.

Yet now he was two hundred feet from the top of Everest. . . .

A travel poster had started it all, more than three years ago. As a junior computer programer in the Applied Physics Division, George Harper knew Dr. Elwin only by sight and by reputation. Even to those working directly under him, Astrotech's brilliant Director of Research was a slightly remote personality, cut off from the ordinary run of men both by his body and by his mind. He was neither liked nor disliked, and, though he was admired and pitied, he was certainly not envied.

Harper, only a few months out of college, doubted if the Doctor even knew of his existence, except as a name on an organization chart. There were ten other programers in the division, all senior to him, and most of them had never exchanged more than a dozen words with their research director. When Harper was co-opted as messenger boy to carry one of the classified files into Dr. Elwin's office, he expected to be in and out with nothing more than a few polite formalities.

That was almost what happened. But just as he was leaving, he was stopped dead by the magnificent panorama of Himalayan peaks covering half of one wall. It had been placed where Dr. Elwin could see it whenever he looked up from his desk, and it showed a scene that Harper knew very well indeed, for he had photographed it himself, as an awed and slightly breathless tourist standing on the trampled snow at the crown of Everest.

There was the white ridge of Kanchenjunga, rearing through the clouds almost a hundred miles away. Nearly in line with it, but much nearer, were the twin peaks of Makalu; and closer still, dominating the foreground, was the immense bulk of Lhotse, Everest's neighbor and rival. Farther around to the west, flowing down valleys so huge that the eye could not appreciate their scale, were the jumbled ice rivers of the Khumbu and Rongbuk glaciers. From this height, their frozen wrinkles looked no larger than the furrows in a plowed field; but those ruts and scars of iron-hard ice were hundreds of feet deep.

Harper was still taking in that spectacular view, reliving old memories, when he heard Dr. Elwin's voice behind him.

"You seem interested. Have you ever been there?"

"Yes, Doctor. My folks took me after I graduated from high school. We stayed at the hotel for a week, and thought we'd have to go home before the weather cleared. But on the last day the wind stopped blowing, and about twenty of us made it to the summit. We were there for an hour, taking pictures of each other."

Dr. Elwin seemed to digest this information for rather a long time. Then he said, in a voice that had lost its previous remoteness and now held a definite undercurrent of excitement: "Sit down, Mr.—ah—Harper. I'd like to hear more."

As he walked back to the chair facing the Director's big uncluttered desk, George Harper found himself somewhat puzzled. What he had done was not in the least unusual; every year thousands of people went to the Hotel Everest, and about a quarter of them reached the mountain's summit. Only last year, in fact, there had been a much-publicized presentation to the ten-thousandth tourist to stand on the top of the world. Some cynics had commented on the extraordinary coincidence that Number 10,000 had just happened to be a rather well-known video starlet.

There was nothing that Harper could tell Dr. Elwin that he couldn't discover just as easily from a dozen other sources —the tourist brochures, for example. However, no young and ambitious scientist would miss this opportunity to impress a man who could do so much to help his career. Harper was neither coldly calculating nor inclined to dabble in office politics, but he knew a good chance when he saw one.

"Well, Doctor," he began, speaking slowly at first as he tried to put his thoughts and memories in order, "the jets land you at a little town called Namchi, about twenty miles from the mountain. Then the bus takes you along a spectacular road up to the hotel, which overlooks the Khumbu Glacier. It's at an altitude of eighteen thousand feet, and there are pressurized rooms for anyone who finds it hard to breathe. Of course, there's a medical staff in attendance, and the management won't accept guests who aren't physically fit. You have to stay at the hotel for at least two days, on a special diet, before you're allowed to go higher.

"From the hotel you can't actually see the summit, because you're too close to the mountain, and it seems to loom right above you. But the view is fantastic. You can see Lhotse and half a dozen other peaks. And it can be scary, too—especially at night. The wind is usually howling somewhere high overhead, and there are weird noises from the moving ice. It's easy to imagine that there are monsters prowling around up in the mountains. . . .

"There's not much to do at the hotel, except to relax and watch the scenery, and to wait until the doctors give you the go-ahead. In the old days it used to take weeks to acclimatize to the thin air; now they can make your blood count shoot up to the right level in forty-eight hours. Even so, about half the visitors—mostly the older ones—decide that this is quite high enough for them.

"What happens next depends on how experienced you are, and how much you're willing to pay. A few expert climbers hire guides and make their own way to the top, using standard mountaineering equipment. That isn't too difficult nowadays, and there are shelters at various strategic spots. Most of these groups make it. But the weather is always a gamble, and every year a few people get killed.

"The average tourist does it the easier way. No aircraft are allowed to land on Everest itself, except in emergencies, but there's a lodge near the crest of Nuptse and a helicopter service to it from the hotel. From the lodge it's only three miles to the summit, via the South Col—an easy climb for anyone in good condition, with a little mountaineering experience. Some people do it without oxygen, though that's not recommended. I kept my mask on until I reached the top; then I took it off and found I could breathe without much difficulty."

"Did you use filters or gas cylinders?"

"Oh, molecular filters—they're quite reliable now, and increase the oxygen concentration over a hundred per cent. They've simplified high-altitude climbing enormously. No one carries compressed gas any more."

"How long did the climb take?"

"A full day. We left just before dawn and were back at nightfall. *That* would have surprised the old-timers. But of course we were starting fresh and traveling light. There are no real problems on the route from the lodge, and steps have been cut at all the tricky places. As I said, it's easy for anyone in good condition."

The instant he repeated those words, Harper wished that he had bitten off his tongue. It seemed incredible that he could have forgotten who he was talking to, but the wonder and excitement of that climb to the top of the world had come back so vividly that for a moment he was once more on that lonely, wind-swept peak. The one spot on Earth where Dr. Elwin could never stand....

But the scientist did not appear to have noticed—or else he was so used to such unthinking tactlessness that it no longer bothered him. Why, wondered Harper, was he so interested in Everest? Probably because of that very inaccessibility; it stood for all that had been denied to him by the accident of birth.

Yet now, only three years later, George Harper paused a bare hundred feet from the summit and drew in the nylon rope as the Doctor caught up with him. Though nothing had ever been said about it, he knew that the scientist wished to be the first to the top. He deserved the honor, and the younger man would do nothing to rob him of it.

"Everything O.K.?" he asked as Dr. Elwin drew abreast of him. The question was quite unnecessary, but Harper felt an urgent need to challenge the great loneliness that now surrounded them. They might have been the only men in all the world; nowhere amid this white wilderness of peaks was there any sign that the human race existed.

Elwin did not answer, but gave an absent-minded nod as he went past, his shining eyes fixed upon the summit. He was walking with a curiously stiff-legged gait, and his feet made remarkably little impression in the snow. And as he walked, there came a faint but unmistakable whine from the bulky backpack he was carrying on his shoulders.

That pack, indeed, was carrying him—or three-quarters of him. As he forged steadily along the last few feet to his once-impossible goal, Dr. Elwin and all his equipment weighed only fifty pounds. And if *that* was still too much, he had only to turn a dial and he would weigh nothing at all.

Here amid the Moon-washed Himalayas was the greatest secret of the twenty-first century. In all the world, there were only five of these experimental Elwin Levitators, and two of them were here on Everest.

Even though he had known about them for two years, and understood something of their basic theory, the "Levvies"—as they had soon been christened at the lab—still seemed like magic to Harper. Their power-packs stored enough electrical energy to lift a two-hundred-and-fifty-pound weight through a vertical distance of ten miles, which gave an ample safety factor for this mission. The lift-and-descend cycle could be repeated almost indefinitely as the units reacted against the Earth's gravitational field. On the way up, the battery discharged; on the way down, it was charged again. Since no mechanical process is completely efficient, there was a slight loss of energy on each cycle, but it could be repeated at least a hundred times before the units were exhausted.

Climbing the mountain with most of their weight neutralized had been an exhilarating experience. The vertical tug of the harness made it feel that they were hanging from invisible balloons, whose buoyancy could be adjusted at will. They needed a certain amount of weight in order to get traction on the ground, and after some experimenting had settled on twenty-five per cent. With this, it was as easy to ascend a one-in-one slope as to walk normally on the level.

Several times they had cut their weight almost to zero to rise hand over hand up vertical rock faces. This had been the strangest experience of all, demanding complete faith in their equipment. To hang suspended in mid-air, apparently supported by nothing but a box of gently humming electronic gear, required a considerable effort of will. But after a few minutes, the sense of power and freedom overcame all fear; for here indeed was the realization of one of man's oldest dreams.

A few weeks ago one of the library staff had found a line from an early twentieth-century poem that described their achievement perfectly: "To ride secure the cruel sky." Not even birds had ever possessed such freedom of the third dimension; this was the *real* conquest of space. The Levitator would open up the mountains and the high places of the world, as a lifetime ago the aqualung had opened up the sea. Once these units had passed their tests and were mass-produced cheaply, every aspect of human civilization would be changed. Transport would be revolutionized. Space travel would be no more expensive than ordinary flying; all mankind would take to the air. What had happened a hundred years earlier with the invention of the automobile was only a mild foretaste of the staggering social and political changes that must now come.

But Dr. Elwin, Harper felt sure, was thinking of none of these in his lonely moment of triumph. Later, he would receive the world's applause (and perhaps its curses), yet it would not mean as much to him as standing here on Earth's highest point. This was truly a victory of mind over matter, of sheer intelligence over a frail and crippled body. All the rest would be anticlimax.

When Harper joined the scientist on the flattened, snow-covered pyramid, they shook hands with rather formal stiffness, because that seemed the right thing to do. But they said nothing; the wonder of their achievement, and the panorama of peaks that stretched as far as the eye could see in every direction, had robbed them of words.

Harper relaxed in the buoyant support of his harness and slowly scanned the circle of the sky. As he recognized them, he mentally called off the names of the surrounding giants: Makalu, Lhotse, Baruntse, Cho Oyu, Kanchenjunga. . . . Even now scores of these peaks had never been climbed. Well, the Levvies would soon change that.

There were many, of course, who would disapprove. But back in the twentieth century there had also been mountaineers who thought it was "cheating" to use oxygen. It was hard to believe that, even after weeks of acclimatization, men had once attempted to reach these heights with no artificial aids at all. Harper remembered Mallory and Irvine, whose bodies still lay undiscovered perhaps within a mile of this very spot.

Behind him, Dr. Elwin cleared his throat.

"Let's go, George," he said quietly, his voice muffled by the oxygen filter. "We must get back before they start looking for us."

With a silent farewell to all those who had stood here before them, they turned away from the summit and started down the gentle slope. The night, which had been brilliantly clear until now, was becoming darker; some high clouds were slipping across the face of the Moon so rapidly that its light switched on and off in a manner that sometimes made it hard to see the route. Harper did not like the look of the weather and began mentally to rearrange their plans. Perhaps it would be better to aim for the shelter on the South Col, rather than attempt to reach the lodge. But he said nothing to Dr. Elwin, not wishing to raise any false alarms.

Now they were moving along a knife edge of rock, with utter darkness on one side and a faintly glimmering snowscape on the other. This would be a terrible place, Harper could not help thinking, to be caught by a storm.

He had barely shaped the thought when the gale was upon them. From out of nowhere, it seemed, came a shrieking blast of air, as if the mountain had been husbanding its strength for this moment. There was no time to do anything; even had they possessed normal weight, they would have been swept off their feet. In seconds, the wind had tossed them out over shadowed, empty blackness.

It was impossible to judge the depths beneath them; when

Harper forced himself to glance down, he could see nothing. Though the wind seemed to be carrying him almost horizontally, he knew that he must be falling. His residual weight would be taking him downward at a quarter of the normal speed. But that would be ample; if they fell four thousand feet, it would be poor consolation to know that it would seem only one thousand.

He had not yet had time for fear—*that* would come later, if he survived—and his main worry, absurdly enough, was that the expensive Levitator might be damaged. He had completely forgotten his partner, for in such a crisis the mind can hold only one idea at a time. The sudden jerk on the nylon rope filled him with puzzled alarm. Then he saw Dr. Elwin slowly revolving around him at the end of the line, like a planet circling a sun.

The sight snapped him back to reality, and to a consciousness of what must be done. His paralysis had probably lasted only a fraction of a second. He shouted across the wind: "Doctor! Use emergency lift!"

As he spoke, he fumbled for the seal on his control unit, tore it open, and pressed the button.

At once, the pack began to hum like a hive of angry bees. He felt the harness tugging at his body as it tried to drag him up into the sky, away from the invisible death below. The simple arithmetic of the Earth's gravitational field blazed in his mind, as if written in letters of fire. One kilowatt could lift a hundred kilograms through a meter every second, and the packs could convert energy at a maximum rate of ten kilowatts—though they could not keep this up for more than a minute. So allowing for his initial weight reduction, he should lift at well over a hundred feet a second.

There was a violent jerk on the rope as the slack between them was taken up. Dr. Elwin had been slow to punch the emergency button, but at last he, too, was ascending. It would be a race between the lifting power of their units and the wind that was sweeping them toward the icy face of Lhotse, now scarcely a thousand feet away.

That wall of snow-streaked rock loomed above them in the

moonlight, a frozen wave of stone. It was impossible to judge their speed accurately, but they could hardly be moving at less than fifty miles an hour. Even if they survived the impact, they could not expect to escape serious injury; and injury here would be as good as death.

Then, just when it seemed that a collision was unavoidable, the current of air suddenly shot skyward, dragging them with it. They cleared the ridge of rock with a comfortable fifty feet to spare. It seemed like a miracle, but, after a dizzying moment of relief, Harper realized that what had saved them was only simple aerodynamics. The wind *had* to rise in order to clear the mountain; on the other side, it would descend again. But that no longer mattered, for the sky ahead was empty.

Now they were moving quietly beneath the broken clouds. Though their speed had not slackened, the roar of the wind had suddenly died away, for they were traveling with it through emptiness. They could even converse comfortably, across the thirty feet of space that still separated them.

"Dr. Elwin," Harper called, "are you O.K.?"

"Yes, George," said the scientist, perfectly calmly. "Now what do we do?"

"We must stop lifting. If we go any higher, we won't be able to breathe—even with the filters."

"You're right. Let's get back into balance."

The angry humming of the packs died to a barely audible electric whine as they cut out the emergency circuits. For a few minutes they yo-yoed up and down on their nylon rope—first one uppermost, then the other—until they managed to get into trim. When they had finally stabilized, they were drifting at a little below thirty thousand feet. Unless the Levvies failed—which, after their overload, was quite possible—they were out of immediate danger.

Their troubles would start when they tried to return to Earth.

No men in all history had ever greeted a stranger dawn. Though they were tired and stiff and cold, and the dryness of the thin air made every breath rasp in their throats, they forgot all these discomforts as the first dim glow spread along the jagged eastern horizon. The stars faded one by one; last to go, only minutes before the moment of daybreak, was the most brilliant of all the space stations—Pacific Number Three, hovering twenty-two thousand miles above Hawaii. Then the sun lifted above a sea of nameless peaks, and the Himalayan day had dawned.

It was like watching sunrise on the Moon. At first, only the highest mountains caught the slanting rays, while the surrounding valleys remained flooded with inky shadows. But slowly the line of light marched down the rocky slopes, and more and more of this harsh, forbidding land climbed into the new day.

Now, if one looked hard enough, it was possible to see signs of human life. There were a few narrow roads, thin columns of smoke from lonely villages, glints of reflected sunlight from monastery roofs. The world below was waking, wholly unaware of the two spectators poised so magically fifteen thousand feet above.

During the night, the wind must have changed direction several times, and Harper had no idea where they were. He could not recognize a single landmark. They could have been anywhere over a five-hundred-mile-long strip of Nepal and Tibet.

The immediate problem was to choose a landing place—and that soon, for they were drifting rapidly toward a jumble of peaks and glaciers where they could hardly expect to find help. The wind was carrying them in a northeasterly direction, toward China. If they floated over the mountains and landed there, it might be weeks before they could get in contact with one of the U.N. Famine Relief Centers and find their way home. They might even be in some personal danger, if they descended out of the sky in an area where there was only an illiterate and superstitious peasant population.

"We'd better get down quickly," said Harper. "I don't like the look of those mountains." His words seemed utterly lost in the void around them. Although Dr. Elwin was only ten feet away, it was easy to imagine that his companion could not hear anything he said. But at last the Doctor nodded his head, in almost reluctant agreement.

"I'm afraid you're right—but I'm not sure we can make it, with this wind. Remember—we can't go down as quickly as we can rise."

That was true enough; the power-packs could be charged at only a tenth of their discharge rate. If they lost altitude and pumped gravitational energy back into them too fast, the cells would overheat and probably explode. The startled Tibetans (or Nepalese?) would think that a large meteorite had detonated in their sky. And no one would ever know exactly what had happened to Dr. Jules Elwin and his promising young assistant.

Five thousand feet above the ground, Harper began to expect the explosion at any moment. They were falling swiftly, but not swiftly enough; very soon they would have to decelerate, lest they hit at too high a speed. To make matters worse, they had completely miscalculated the air speed at ground level. That infernal, unpredictable wind was blowing a near-gale once more. They could see streamers of snow, torn from exposed ridges, waving like ghostly banners beneath them. While they had been moving with the wind, they were unaware of its power; now they must once again make the dangerous transition between stubborn rock and softly yielding sky.

The air current was funneling them into the mouth of a canyon. There was no chance of lifting above it. They were committed, and would have to choose the best landing place they could find.

The canyon was narrowing at a fearsome rate. Now it was little more than a vertical cleft, and the rocky walls were sliding past at thirty or forty miles an hour. From time to time random eddies would swing them to the right, then the left; often they missed collisions by only a few feet. Once, when they were sweeping scant yards above a ledge thickly covered with snow, Harper was tempted to pull the quick-release that would jettison the Levitator. But that would be jumping from the frying pan into the fire: they might get safely back onto firm ground only to find themselves trapped unknown miles from all possibility of help.

Yet even at this moment of renewed peril, he felt very little fear. It was all like an exciting dream—a dream from which he would presently wake up to find himself safely in his own bed. This fantastic adventure could not really be happening to him. . . .

"George!" shouted the Doctor. "Now's our chance—if we can snag that boulder!"

They had only seconds in which to act. At once, they both began to play out the nylon rope, until it hung in a great loop beneath them, its lowest portion only a yard above the racing ground. A large rock, some twenty feet high, lay exactly in their line of flight; beyond it, a wide patch of snow gave promise of a reasonably soft landing.

The rope skittered over the lower curves of the boulder, seemed about to slip clear, then caught beneath an overhang. Harper felt the sudden jerk. He was swung around like a stone on the end of a sling.

I never thought that snow could be so hard, he told himself. After that there was a brief and brilliant explosion of light; then nothing.

He was back at the university, in the lecture room. One of the professors was talking, in a voice that was familiar, yet somehow did not seem to belong here. In a sleepy, halfhearted fashion, he ran through the names of his college instructors. No, it was certainly none of them. Yet he knew the voice so well, and it was undoubtedly lecturing to *someone.*

". . . still quite young when I realized that there was something wrong with Einstein's Theory of Gravitation. In particular, there seemed to be a fallacy underlying the Principle of Equivalence. According to this, there is no way of distinguishing between the effects produced by gravitation and those of acceleration.

"But this is clearly false. One can create a uniform acceleration; but a uniform gravitational field is impossible, since it obeys an inverse square law, and therefore must vary even over quite short distances. So tests can easily be devised to distinguish between the two cases, and this made me wonder if . . ."

The softly spoken words left no more impression on Harper's mind than if they were in a foreign language. He realized dimly that he *should* understand all this, but it was too much trouble to look for the meaning. Anyway, the first problem was to decide where he was.

Unless there was something wrong with his eyes, he was in complete darkness. He blinked, and the effort brought on such a splitting headache that he gave a cry of pain.

"George! Are you all right?"

Of course! That had been Dr. Elwin's voice, talking softly there in the darkness. But talking to *whom?*

"I've got a terrible headache. And there's a pain in my side when I try to move. What's happened? Why is it dark?"

"You've had concussion—and I think you've cracked a rib. Don't do any unnecessary talking. You've been unconscious all day. It's night again, and we're inside the tent. I'm saving our batteries."

The glare from the flashlight was almost blinding when Dr. Elwin switched it on, and Harper saw the walls of the tiny tent around them. How lucky that they had brought full mountaineering equipment, just in case they got trapped on Everest. But perhaps it would only prolong the agony. . . .

He was surprised that the crippled scientist had managed, without any assistance, to unpack all their gear, erect the tent, and drag him inside. Everything was laid out neatly: the first-aid kit, the concentrated-food cans, the water containers, the tiny red gas cylinders for the portable stove. Only the bulky Levitator units were missing; presumably they had been left outside to give more room.

"You were talking to someone when I woke up," Harper said. "Or was I dreaming?" Though the indirect light reflected from the walls of the tent made it hard to read the other's expression, he could see that Elwin was embarrassed. Instantly, he knew why, and wished that he had never asked the question.

The scientist did not believe that they would survive. He had been recording his notes, in case their bodies were ever discovered. Harper wondered bleakly if he had already recorded his last will and testament.

Before Elwin could answer, he quickly changed the subject. "Have you called Lifeguard?"

"I've been trying every half hour, but I'm afraid we're shielded by the mountains. I can hear them, but they don't receive us."

Dr. Elwin picked up the little recorder-transceiver, which he had unstrapped from its normal place on his wrist, and switched it on.

"This is Lifeguard Four," said a faint mechanical voice, "listening out now."

During the five-second pause, Elwin pressed the SOS button, then waited.

"This is Lifeguard Four, listening out now."

They waited for a full minute, but there was no acknowledgment of their call. Well, Harper told himself grimly, it's too late to start blaming each other now. Several times while they had been drifting above the mountains they had debated whether to call the global rescue service, but had decided against it, partly because there seemed no point in doing so while they were still air-borne, partly because of the unavoidable publicity that would follow. It was easy to be wise after the event: who would have dreamed that they would land in one of the few places beyond Lifeguard's reach?

Dr. Elwin switched off the transceiver, and the only sound in the little tent was the faint moaning of the wind along the mountain walls within which they were doubly trapped—beyond escape, beyond communication.

"Don't worry," he said at last. "By morning, we'll think of a way out. There's nothing we can do until dawn—except make ourselves comfortable. So drink some of this hot soup."

•

Several hours later, the headache no longer bothered Harper. Though he suspected that a rib was indeed cracked, he had found a position that was comfortable as long as he did not move, and he felt almost at peace with the world.

He had passed through successive phases of despair, anger at Dr. Elwin, and self-recrimination at having become involved in such a crazy enterprise. Now he was calm again, though his mind, searching for ways of escape, was too active to allow sleep.

Outside the tent, the wind had almost died away, and the night was very still. It was no longer completely dark, for the Moon had risen. Though its direct rays would never reach them here, there must be some reflected light from the snows above. Harper could just make out a dim glow at the very threshold of vision, seeping through the translucent heat-retaining walls of the tent.

First of all, he told himself, they were in no immediate danger. The food would last for at least a week; there was plenty of snow that could be melted to provide water. In a day or two, if his rib behaved itself, they might be able to take off again—this time, he hoped, with happier results.

From not far away there came a curious, soft thud, which puzzled Harper until he realized that a mass of snow must have fallen somewhere. The night was now so extraordinarily quiet that he almost imagined he could hear his own heartbeat; every breath of his sleeping companion seemed unnaturally loud.

Curious, how the mind was distracted by trivialities! He turned his thoughts back to the problem of survival. Even if he was not fit enough to move, the Doctor could attempt the flight by himself. This was a case where one man would have just as good a chance of success as two.

There was another of those soft thuds, slightly louder this time. It was a little odd, Harper thought fleetingly, for snow to move in the cold stillness of the night. He hoped that there was no risk of a slide; having had no time for a clear view of their landing place, he could not assess the danger. He wondered if he should awaken the Doctor, who must have had a good look around before he erected the tent. Then, fatalistically, he decided against it; if there *was* an impending avalanche, it was not likely that they could do much to escape.

Back to problem number one. Here was an interesting solution well worth considering. They could attach the transceiver to one of the Levvies and send the whole thing aloft. The signal would be picked up as soon as the unit left the canyon, and Lifeguard would find them within a few hours—or, at the very most, a few days.

Of course, it would mean sacrificing one of the Levvies, and if nothing came of it, they would be in an even worse plight. But all the same . . .

What was that? This was no soft thudding of loose snow. It was a faint but unmistakable "click," as of one pebble knocking against another. And pebbles did not move themselves.

You're imagining things, Harper told himself. The idea of anyone, or anything, moving around one of the high Himalayan passes in the middle of the night was completely ridiculous. But his throat became suddenly dry, and he felt the flesh crawl at the back of his neck. He had heard *something,* and it was impossible to argue it away.

Damn the Doctor's breathing; it was so noisy that it was hard to focus on any sounds from outside. Did this mean that Dr. Elwin, fast asleep though he was, had also been alerted by his ever-watchful subconscious? He was being fanciful again. . . .

Click.

Perhaps it was a little closer. It certainly came from a different direction. It was almost as if something—moving with uncanny but not complete silence—was slowly circling the tent.

This was the moment when George Harper devoutly wished he had never heard of the Abominable Snowman. It was true that he knew little enough about it, but that little was far too much.

He remembered that the Yeti, as the Nepalese called it, had

been a persistent Himalayan myth for more than a hundred years. A dangerous monster larger than a man, it had never been captured, photographed, or even described by reputable witnesses. Most Westerners were quite certain that it was pure fantasy, and were totally unconvinced by the scanty evidence of tracks in the snow, or patches of skin preserved in obscure monasteries. The mountain tribesmen knew better. And now Harper was afraid that they were right.

Then, when nothing more happened for long seconds, his fears began slowly to dissolve. Perhaps his overwrought imagination had been playing tricks; in the circumstances, that would hardly be surprising. With a deliberate and determined effort of will, he turned his thoughts once more toward the problem of rescue. He was making fair progress when something bumped into the tent.

Only the fact that his throat muscles were paralyzed from sheer fright prevented him from yelling. He was utterly unable to move. Then, in the darkness beside him, he heard Dr. Elwin begin to stir sleepily.

"What is it?" muttered the scientist. "Are you all right?"

Harper felt his companion turn over and knew that he was groping for the flashlight. He wanted to whisper: "For God's sake, keep quiet!" but no words could escape his parched lips. There was a click, and the beam of the flashlight formed a brilliant circle on the wall of the tent.

That wall was now bowed in toward them as if a heavy weight was resting upon it. And in the center of the bulge was a completely unmistakable pattern: the imprint of a distorted hand or claw. It was only about two feet from the ground; whatever was outside seemed to be kneeling, as it fumbled at the fabric of the tent.

The light must have disturbed it, for the imprint abruptly vanished, and the tent wall sprang flat once more. There was a low, snarling growl; then, for a long time, silence.

Harper found that he was breathing again. At any moment he had expected the tent to tear open, and some unimaginable horror to come rushing in upon them. Instead, almost anticlimactically, there was only a faint and far-off wailing from a transient gust of wind in the mountains high above. He felt himself shivering uncontrollably; it had nothing to do with the temperature, for it was comfortably warm in their little insulated world.

Then there came a familiar—indeed, almost friendly—sound. It was the metallic ring of an empty can striking on stone, and it somehow relaxed the tension a little. For the first time, Harper found himself able to speak, or at least to whisper.

"It's found our food containers. Perhaps it'll go away now."

Almost as if in reply, there was a low snarl that seemed to convey anger and disappointment, then the sound of a blow, and the clatter of cans rolling away into the darkness. Harper suddenly remembered that all the food was here in the tent; only the discarded empties were outside. That was not a cheerful thought. He wished that, like superstitious tribesmen, they had left an offering for whatever gods or demons the mountains could conjure forth.

What happened next was so sudden, so utterly unexpected, that it was all over before he had time to react. There was a scuffling sound, as of something being banged against rock; then a familiar electric whine; then a startled grunt.

And then, a heart-stopping scream of rage and frustration that turned swiftly to sheer terror and began to dwindle away at ever-increasing speed, up, up, into the empty sky.

The fading sound triggered the one appropriate memory in Harper's mind. Once he had seen an early-twentieth-century movie on the history of flight, and it had contained a ghastly sequence showing a dirigible launching. Some of the ground crew had hung on to the mooring lines just a few seconds too long, and the airship had dragged them up into the sky, dangling helplessly beneath it. Then, one by one, they had lost their hold and dropped back to the earth.

Harper waited for a distant thud, but it never came. Then he realized that the Doctor was saying, over and over again: "I left the two units tied together. I left the two units tied together."

He was still in too much of a state of shock for even that information to worry him. Instead, all he felt was a detached and admirably scientific sense of disappointment.

Now he would never know what it was that had been prowling around their tent, in the lonely hours before the Himalayan dawn.

One of the mountain rescue helicopters, flown by a skeptical Sikh who still wondered if the whole thing was an elaborate joke, came nosing down the canyon in the late afternoon. By the time the machine had landed in a flurry of snow, Dr. Elwin was already waving frantically with one arm and supporting himself on the tent framework with the other.

As he recognized the crippled scientist, the helicopter pilot felt a sensation of almost superstitious awe. So the report *must* be true; there was no other way in which Elwin could possibly have reached this place. And that meant that everything flying in and above the skies of Earth was, from this moment, as obsolete as an ox-cart.

"Thank God you found us," said the Doctor, with heartfelt gratitude. "How did you get here so quickly?"

"You can thank the radar tracking networks, and the telescopes in the orbital met stations. We'd have been here earlier, but at first we thought it was all a hoax."

"I don't understand."

"What would *you* have said, Doctor, if someone reported a very dead Himalayan snow leopard mixed up in a tangle of straps and boxes—and holding constant altitude at ninety thousand feet?"

Inside the tent, George Harper started to laugh, despite the pain it caused. The Doctor put his head through the flap and asked anxiously: "What's the matter?"

"Nothing—ouch. But I was wondering how we are going to get the poor beast down, before it's a menace to navigation."

"Oh, someone will have to go up with another Levvy and press the buttons. Maybe we should have a radio control on all units. . . ."

Dr. Elwin's voice faded out in mid-sentence. Already he

was far away, lost in dreams that would change the face of many worlds.

In a little while he would come down from the mountains, a later Moses bearing the laws of a new civilization. For he would give back to all mankind the freedom lost so long ago, when the first amphibians left their weightless home beneath the waves.

The billion-year battle against the force of gravity was over.

November 1966

Neutron Tide

"In deference to the next of kin," Commander Cummerbund explained with morbid relish, "the full story of the supercruiser *Flatbush*'s last mission has never been revealed. You know, of course, that she was lost during the war against the Mucoids."

We all shuddered. Even now, the very name of the gelatinous monsters who had come slurping Earthward from the general direction of the Coal Sack aroused vomitive memories.

"I knew her skipper well—Captain Karl van Rinderpest, hero of the final assault on the unspeakable, but not unshriekable, ! ! Yeetch."

He paused politely to let us unplug our ears and mop up our spilled drinks.

"*Flatbush* had just launched a salvo of probability inverters against the Mucoid home planet and was heading back toward deep space in formation with three destroyers—the Russian *Lieutenant Kizhe,* the Israeli *Chutzpah,* and Her Majesty's *Insufferable.* They were still accelerating when a fantastically unlikely accident occurred. *Flatbush* ran straight into the gravity well of a neutron star."

When our expressions of horror and incredulity had subsided, he continued gravely.

"Yes—a sphere of ultimately condensed matter, only ten miles across, yet as massive as a sun—and hence with a surface gravity one hundred billion times that of Earth.

"The other ships were lucky. They only skirted the outer fringe of the field and managed to escape, though their orbits were deflected almost a hundred and eighty degrees. But *Flatbush,* we calculated later, must have passed within a few dozen miles of that unthinkable concentration of mass, and so experienced the full violence of its tidal forces.

"Now in any reasonable gravitational field—even that of a White Dwarf, which may run up to a million Earth g's—you just swing around the center of attraction and head on out into space again, without feeling a thing. At the closest point you could be accelerating at hundreds or thousands of g's—but you're still in free fall, so there are no physical effects. Sorry if I'm laboring the obvious, but I realize that everyone here isn't technically orientated."

If this was intended as a crack at Fleet Paymaster General "Sticky Fingers" Geldclutch, he never noticed, being well into his fifth beaker of Martian Joy Juice.

"For a neutron star, however, this is no longer true. Near the center of mass the gravitational gradient—that is, the rate at which the field changes with distance—is so enormous that even across the width of a small body like a spaceship there can be a difference of a hundred thousand g's. I need hardly tell you what *that* sort of field can do to any material object.

"*Flatbush* must have been torn to pieces almost instantly, and the pieces themselves must have flowed like liquid during the few seconds they took to swing around the star. Then the fragments headed on out into space again.

"Months later a radar sweep by the Salvage Corps located some of the debris. I've seen it—surrealistically shaped lumps of the toughest metals we possess twisted together like taffy. And there was only one item that could even be recognized—it must have come from some unfortunate engineer's tool kit."

The Commander's voice dropped almost to inaudibility, and he dashed away a manly tear.

"I really hate to say this." He sighed. "But the only identifiable fragment of the pride of the United States Space Navy was—one star-mangled spanner."

January 1970

Transit of Earth

Testing, one, two, three, four, five . . .

Evans speaking. I will continue to record as long as possible. This is a two-hour capsule, but I doubt if I'll fill it.

That photograph has haunted me all my life; now, too late, I know why. (But would it have made any difference if I *had* known? That's one of those meaningless and unanswerable questions the mind keeps returning to endlessly, like the tongue exploring a broken tooth.)

I've not seen it for years, but I've only to close my eyes and I'm back in a landscape almost as hostile—and as beautiful—as this one. Fifty million miles sunward, and seventy-two years in the past, five men face the camera amid the antarctic snows. Not even the bulky furs can hide the exhaustion and defeat that mark every line of their bodies; and their faces are already touched by Death.

There were five of them. There were five of us, and of course we also took a group photograph. But everything else was different. We were smiling—cheerful, confident. And our picture was on all the screens of Earth within ten minutes. It was months before *their* camera was found and brought back to civilization.

And we die in comfort, with all modern conveniences—including many that Robert Falcon Scott could never have imagined, when he stood at the South Pole in 1912.

Two hours later. I'll start giving exact times when it becomes important.

All the facts are in the log, and by now the whole world knows them. So I guess I'm doing this largely to settle my mind—to talk myself into facing the inevitable. The trouble is, I'm not sure what subjects to avoid, and which to tackle head on. Well, there's only one way to find out.

The first item: in twenty-four hours, at the very most, all the oxygen will be gone. That leaves me with the three classical choices. I can let the carbon dioxide build up until I become unconscious. I can step outside and crack the suit, leaving Mars to do the job in about two minutes. Or I can use one of the tablets in the med kit.

CO_2 build-up. Everyone says that's quite easy—just like going to sleep. I've no doubt that's true; unfortunately, in my case it's associated with nightmare number one. . . .

I wish I'd never come across that damn book *True Stories of World War Two,* or whatever it was called. There was one chapter about a German submarine, found and salvaged after the war. The crew was still inside it—*two* men per bunk. And between each pair of skeletons, the single respirator set they'd been sharing. . . .

Well, at least that won't happen here. But I know, with a deadly certainty, that as soon as I find it hard to breathe, I'll be back in that doomed U-boat.

So what about the quicker way? When you're exposed to vacuum, you're unconscious in ten or fifteen seconds, and people who've been through it say it's not painful—just peculiar. But trying to breathe something that isn't there brings me altogether too neatly to nightmare number two.

This time, it's a personal experience. As a kid, I used to do a lot of skin diving, when my family went to the Caribbean for vacations. There was an old freighter that had sunk twenty years before, out on a reef, with its deck only a couple of yards below the surface. Most of the hatches were open, so it was easy to get inside, to look for souvenirs and hunt the big fish that like to shelter in such places.

Of course it was dangerous if you did it without scuba gear. So what boy could resist the challenge?

My favorite route involved diving into a hatch on the foredeck, swimming about fifty feet along a passageway dimly lit by portholes a few yards apart, then angling up a short flight of stairs and emerging through a door in the battered superstructure. The whole trip took less than a minute—an easy dive for anyone in good condition. There was even time to do some sight-seeing, or to play with a few fish along the route. And sometimes, for a change, I'd switch directions, going in the door and coming out again through the hatch.

That was the way I did it the last time. I hadn't dived for a week—there had been a big storm, and the sea was too rough—so I was impatient to get going.

I deep-breathed on the surface for about two minutes, until I felt the tingling in my finger tips that told me it was time to stop. Then I jackknifed and slid gently down toward the black rectangle of the open doorway.

It always looked ominous and menacing—that was part of the thrill. And for the first few yards I was almost completely blind; the contrast between the tropical glare above water and the gloom between decks was so great that it took quite a while for my eyes to adjust. Usually, I was halfway along the corridor before I could see anything clearly. Then the illumination would steadily increase as I approached the open hatch, where a shaft of sunlight would paint a dazzling rectangle on the rusty, barnacled metal floor.

I'd almost made it when I realized that, this time, the light wasn't getting better. There was no slanting column of sunlight ahead of me, leading up to the world of air and life.

I had a second of baffled confusion, wondering if I'd lost my way. Then I knew what had happened—and confusion turned into sheer panic. Sometime during the storm, the hatch must have slammed shut. It weighed at least a quarter of a ton.

I don't remember making a U turn; the next thing I recall is swimming quite slowly back along the passage and telling myself: Don't hurry; your air will last longer if you take it easy. I could see very well now, because my eyes had had plenty of time to become dark-adapted. There were lots of details I'd never noticed before, like the red squirrelfish lurking in the shadows, the green fronds and algae growing in the little patches of light around the portholes, and even a single rubber boot, apparently in excellent condition, lying where someone must have kicked it off. And once, out of a side corridor, I noticed a big grouper staring at me with bulbous eyes, his thick lips half parted, as if he was astonished at my intrusion.

The band around my chest was getting tighter and tighter. It was impossible to hold my breath any longer. Yet the stairway still seemed an infinite distance ahead. I let some bubbles of air dribble out of my mouth. That improved matters for a moment, but, once I had exhaled, the ache in my lungs became even more unendurable.

Now there was no point in conserving strength by flippering along with that steady, unhurried stroke. I snatched the ultimate few cubic inches of air from my face mask—feeling it flatten against my nose as I did so—and swallowed them down into my starving lungs. At the same time, I shifted gear and drove forward with every last atom of strength. . . .

And that's all I remember until I found myself spluttering and coughing in the daylight, clinging to the broken stub of the mast. The water around me was stained with blood, and I wondered why. Then, to my great surprise, I noticed a deep gash in my right calf. I must have banged into some sharp obstruction, but I'd never noticed it and even then felt no pain.

That was the end of my skin diving until I started astronaut training ten years later and went into the underwater zero-gee simulator. Then it was different, because I was using scuba gear. But I had some nasty moments that I was afraid the psychologists would notice, and I always made sure that I got nowhere near emptying my tank. Having nearly suffocated once, I'd no intention of risking it again. . . .

I know exactly what it will feel like to breathe the freezing wisp of near-vacuum that passes for atmosphere on Mars. No thank you.

So what's wrong with poison? Nothing, I suppose. The

stuff we've got takes only fifteen seconds, they told us. But all my instincts are against it, even when there's no sensible alternative.

Did Scott have poison with him? I doubt it. And if he did, I'm sure he never used it.

I'm not going to replay this. I hope it's been of some use, but I can't be sure.

The radio has just printed out a message from Earth, reminding me that transit starts in two hours. As if I'm likely to forget—when four men have already died so that I can be the first human being to see it. And the only one, for exactly a hundred years. It isn't often that Sun, Earth, and Mars line up neatly like this; the last time was in 1905, when poor old Lowell was still writing his beautiful nonsense about the canals and the great dying civilization that had built them. Too bad it was all delusion.

I'd better check the telescope and the timing equipment.

The Sun is quiet today—as it should be, anyway, near the middle of the cycle. Just a few small spots, and some minor areas of disturbance around them. The solar weather is set calm for months to come. That's one thing the others won't have to worry about, on their way home.

I think that was the worst moment, watching *Olympus* lift off Phobos and head back to Earth. Even though we'd known for weeks that nothing could be done, that was the final closing of the door.

It was night, and we could see everything perfectly. Phobos had come leaping up out of the west a few hours earlier, and was doing its mad backward rush across the sky, growing from a tiny crescent to a half-moon; before it reached the zenith it would disappear as it plunged into the shadow of Mars and became eclipsed.

We'd been listening to the countdown, of course, trying to go about our normal work. It wasn't easy, accepting at last the fact that fifteen of us had come to Mars and only ten would return. Even then, I suppose there were millions back on Earth who still could not understand. They must have found it impossible to believe that *Olympus* couldn't descend a mere four thousand miles to pick us up. The Space Administration had been bombarded with crazy rescue schemes; heaven knows, we'd thought of enough ourselves. But when the permafrost under Landing Pad Three finally gave way and *Pegasus* toppled, that was that. It still seems a miracle that the ship didn't blow up when the propellant tank ruptured. . . .

I'm wandering again. Back to Phobos and the countdown.

On the telescope monitor, we could clearly see the fissured plateau where *Olympus* had touched down after we'd separated and begun our own descent. Though our friends would never land on Mars, at least they'd had a little world of their own to explore; even for a satellite as small as Phobos, it worked out at thirty square miles per man. A lot of territory to search for strange minerals and debris from space—or to carve your name so that future ages would know that you were the first of all men to come this way.

The ship was clearly visible as a stubby, bright cylinder against the dull-gray rocks; from time to time some flat surface would catch the light of the swiftly moving sun, and would flash with mirror brilliance. But about five minutes before lift-off, the picture became suddenly pink, then crimson—then vanished completely as Phobos rushed into eclipse.

The countdown was still at ten seconds when we were startled by a blast of light. For a moment, we wondered if *Olympus* had also met with catastrophe. Then we realized that someone was filming the take-off, and the external floodlights had been switched on.

During those last few seconds, I think we all forgot our own predicament; we were up there aboard *Olympus,* willing the thrust to build up smoothly and lift the ship out of the tiny gravitational field of Phobos, and then away from Mars for the long fall sunward. We heard Commander Richmond say "Ignition," there was a brief burst of interference, and the patch of light began to move in the field of the telescope.

That was all. There was no blazing column of fire, because, of course, there's really no ignition when a nuclear rocket lights up. "Lights up" indeed! That's another hangover from the old chemical technology. But a hot hydrogen blast is completely invisible; it seems a pity that we'll never again see anything so spectacular as a Saturn or a Korolov blast-off.

Just before the end of the burn, *Olympus* left the shadow of Mars and burst out into sunlight again, reappearing almost instantly as a brilliant, swiftly moving star. The blaze of light must have startled them aboard the ship, because we heard someone call out: "Cover that window!" Then, a few seconds later, Richmond announced: "Engine cutoff." Whatever happened, *Olympus* was now irrevocably headed back to Earth.

A voice I didn't recognize—though it must have been the Commander's—said "Good-by, *Pegasus*," and the radio transmission switched off. There was, of course, no point in saying "Good luck." *That* had all been settled weeks ago.

I've just played this back. Talking of luck, there's been one compensation, though not for us. With a crew of only ten, *Olympus* has been able to dump a third of her expendables and lighten herself by several tons. So now she'll get home a month ahead of schedule.

Plenty of things could have gone wrong in that month; we may yet have saved the expedition. Of course, we'll never know—but it's a nice thought.

I've been playing a lot of music, full blast—now that there's no one else to be disturbed. Even if there were any Martians, I don't suppose this ghost of an atmosphere can carry the sound more than a few yards.

We have a fine collection, but I have to choose carefully. Nothing downbeat and nothing that demands too much concentration. Above all, nothing with human voices. So I restrict myself to the lighter orchestral classics; the "New World" symphony and Grieg's piano concerto fill the bill perfectly. At the moment I'm listening to Rachmaninoff's "Rhapsody on a Theme of Paganini," but now I must switch off and get down to work.

There are only five minutes to go. All the equipment is in perfect condition. The telescope is tracking the Sun, the video recorder is standing by, the precision timer is running.

These observations will be as accurate as I can make them. I owe it to my lost comrades, whom I'll soon be joining. They gave me their oxygen, so that I can still be alive at this moment. I hope you remember that, a hundred or a thousand years from now, whenever you crank these figures into the computers. . . .

Only a minute to go; getting down to business. For the record: year, 1984; month, May; day, 11, coming up to four hours thirty minutes Ephemeris Time . . . *now*.

Half a minute to contact. Switching recorder and timer to high speed. Just rechecked position angle to make sure I'm looking at the right spot on the Sun's limb. Using power of five hundred—image perfectly steady even at this low elevation.

Four thirty-two. Any moment now . . .

There it is . . . there it is! I can hardly believe it! A tiny black dent in the edge of the Sun . . . growing, growing, growing . . .

Hello, Earth. Look up at me, the brightest star in your sky, straight overhead at midnight. . . .

Recorder back to slow.

Four thirty-five. It's as if a thumb is pushing into the Sun's edge, deeper and deeper. . . . Fascinating to watch . . .

Four forty-one. Exactly halfway. The Earth's a perfect black semicircle—a clean bite out of the Sun. As if some disease is eating it away . . .

Four forty-eight. Ingress three-quarters complete.

Four hours forty-nine minutes thirty seconds. Recorder on high speed again.

The line of contact with the Sun's edge is shrinking fast. Now it's a barely visible black thread. In a few seconds, the whole Earth will be superimposed on the Sun.

Now I can see the effects of the atmosphere. There's a thin

halo of light surrounding that black hole in the Sun. Strange to think that I'm seeing the glow of all the sunsets—and all the sunrises—that are taking place around the whole Earth at this very moment. . . .

Ingress complete—four hours fifty minutes five seconds. The whole world has moved onto the face of the Sun. A perfectly circular black disc silhouetted against that inferno ninety million miles below. It looks bigger than I expected; one could easily mistake it for a fair-sized sunspot.

Nothing more to see now for six hours, when the Moon appears, trailing Earth by half the Sun's width. I'll beam the recorder data back to Lunacom, then try to get some sleep.

My very last sleep. Wonder if I'll need drugs. It seems a pity to waste these last few hours, but I want to conserve my strength—and my oxygen.

I think it was Dr. Johnson who said that nothing settles a man's mind so wonderfully as the knowledge that he'll be hanged in the morning. How the hell did *he* know?

Ten hours thirty minutes Ephemeris Time. Dr. Johnson was right. I had only one pill, and don't remember any dreams.

The condemned man also ate a hearty breakfast. Cut that out . . .

Back at the telescope. Now the Earth's halfway across the disc, passing well north of center. In ten minutes, I should see the Moon.

I've just switched to the highest power of the telescope—two thousand. The image is slightly fuzzy, but still fairly good; atmospheric halo very distinct. I'm hoping to see the cities on the dark side of Earth. . . .

No luck. Probably too many clouds. A pity; it's theoretically possible, but we never succeeded. I wish . . . never mind.

Ten hours forty minutes. Recorder on slow speed. Hope I'm looking at the right spot.

Fifteen seconds to go. Recorder fast.

Damn—missed it. Doesn't matter—the recorder will have caught the exact moment. There's a little black notch already in the side of the Sun. First contact must have been about ten hours forty-one minutes twenty seconds ET.

What a long way it is between Earth and Moon; there's half the width of the Sun between them. You wouldn't think the two bodies had anything to do with each other. Makes you realize just how big the Sun really is. . . .

Ten hours forty-four minutes. The Moon's exactly halfway over the edge. A very small, very clear-cut semicircular bite out of the edge of the Sun.

Ten hours forty-seven minutes five seconds. Internal contact. The Moon's clear of the edge, entirely inside the Sun. Don't suppose I can see anything on the night side, but I'll increase the power.

That's funny.

Well, well. Someone must be trying to talk to me; there's a tiny light pulsing away there on the darkened face of the moon. Probably the laser at Imbrium Base.

Sorry, everyone. I've said all my good-byes, and don't want to go through that again. Nothing can be important now.

Still, it's almost hypnotic—that flickering point of light, coming out of the face of the Sun itself. Hard to believe that, even after it's traveled all this distance, the beam is only a hundred miles wide. Lunacom's going to all this trouble to aim it exactly at me, and I suppose I should feel guilty at ignoring it. But I don't. I've nearly finished my work, and the things of Earth are no longer any concern of mine.

Ten hours fifty minutes. Recorder off. That's it—until the end of Earth transit, two hours from now.

I've had a snack and am taking my last look at the view from the observation bubble. The Sun's still high, so there's not much contrast, but the light brings out all the colors vividly—the countless varieties of red and pink and crimson, so startling against the deep blue of the sky. How different from the Moon—though that, too, has its own beauty.

It's strange how surprising the obvious can be. Everyone knew that Mars was red. But we didn't really expect the red of rust, the red of blood. Like the Painted Desert of Arizona; after a while, the eye longs for green.

To the north, there is one welcome change of color; the cap of carbon-dioxide snow on Mount Burroughs is a dazzling white pyramid. That's another surprise. Burroughs is twenty-five thousand feet above Mean Datum; when I was a boy, there weren't supposed to be any mountains on Mars. . . .

The nearest sand dune is a quarter of a mile away, and it, too, has patches of frost on its shaded slope. During the last storm, we thought it moved a few feet, but we couldn't be sure. Certainly the dunes *are* moving, like those on Earth. One day, I suppose, this base will be covered—only to reappear again in a thousand years. Or ten thousand.

That strange group of rocks—the Elephant, the Capitol, the Bishop—still holds its secrets, and teases me with the memory of our first big disappointment. We could have sworn that they were sedimentary; how eagerly we rushed out to look for fossils! Even now, we don't know what formed that outcropping. The geology of Mars is still a mass of contradictions and enigmas. . . .

We have passed on enough problems to the future, and those who come after us will find many more. But there's one mystery we never reported to Earth, or even entered in the log. . . .

The first night after we landed, we took turns keeping watch. Brennan was on duty, and woke me up soon after midnight. I was annoyed—it was ahead of time—and then he told me that he'd seen a light moving around the base of the Capitol.

We watched for at least an hour, until it was my turn to take over. But we saw nothing; whatever that light was, it never reappeared.

Now Brennan was as levelheaded and unimaginative as they come; if he said he saw a light, then he saw one. Maybe it was some kind of electric discharge, or the reflection of

Phobos on a piece of sand-polished rock. Anyway, we decided not to mention it to Lunacom, unless we saw it again.

Since I've been alone, I've often awakened in the night and looked out toward the rocks. In the feeble illumination of Phobos and Deimos, they remind me of the skyline of a darkened city. And it has always remained darkened. No lights have ever appeared for me. . . .

Twelve hours forty-nine minutes Ephemeris Time. The last act's about to begin. Earth has nearly reached the edge of the Sun. The two narrow horns of light that still embrace it are barely touching. . . .

Recorder on fast.

Contact! Twelve hours fifty minutes sixteen seconds. The crescents of light no longer meet. A tiny black spot has appeared at the edge of the Sun, as the Earth begins to cross it. It's growing longer, longer. . . .

Recorder on slow. Eighteen minutes to wait before Earth finally clears the face of the Sun.

The Moon still has more than halfway to go; it's not yet reached the mid-point of its transit. It looks like a little round blob of ink, only a quarter the size of Earth. And there's no light flickering there any more. Lunacom must have given up.

Well, I have just a quarter of an hour left, here in my last home. Time seems to be accelerating the way it does in the final minutes before a lift-off. No matter; I have everything worked out now. I can even relax.

Already, I feel part of history. I am one with Captain Cook, back in Tahiti in 1769, watching the transit of Venus. Except for that image of the Moon trailing along behind, it must have looked just like this. . . .

What would Cook have thought, over two hundred years ago, if he'd known that one day a man would observe the whole Earth in transit from an outer world? I'm sure he would have been astonished—and then delighted. . . .

But I feel a closer identity with a man not yet born. I hope you hear these words, whoever you may be. Perhaps you will be standing on this very spot, a hundred years from now, when the next transit occurs.

Greetings to 2084, November 10! I wish you better luck than we had. I suppose you will have come here on a luxury liner. Or you may have been born on Mars, and be a stranger to Earth. You will know things that I cannot imagine. Yet somehow I don't envy you. I would not even change places with you if I could.

For you will remember my name, and know that I was the first of all mankind ever to see a transit of Earth. And no one will see another for a hundred years. . . .

Twelve hours fifty-nine minutes. Exactly halfway through egress. The Earth is a perfect semicircle—a black shadow on the face of the Sun. I still can't escape from the impression that something has taken a big bite out of that golden disc. In nine minutes it will be gone, and the Sun will be whole again.

Thirteen hours seven minutes. Recorder on fast.

Earth has almost gone. There's just a shallow black dimple at the edge of the Sun. You could easily mistake it for a small spot, going over the limb.

Thirteen hours eight.

Good-by, beautiful Earth.

Going, going, going. Good-by, good—

I'm O.K. again now. The timings have all been sent home on the beam. In five minutes, they'll join the accumulated wisdom of mankind. And Lunacom will know that I stuck to my post.

But I'm not sending this. I'm going to leave it here, for the next expedition—whenever that may be. It could be ten or twenty years before anyone comes here again. No point in going back to an old site when there's a whole world waiting to be explored. . . .

So this capsule will stay here, as Scott's diary remained in his tent, until the next visitors find it. But they won't find me.

Strange how hard it is to get away from Scott. I think he gave me the idea.

For his body will not lie frozen forever in the Antarctic, isolated from the great cycle of life and death. Long ago, that lonely tent began its march to the sea. Within a few years, it was buried by the falling snow and had become part of the glacier that crawls eternally away from the Pole. In a few brief centuries, the sailor will have returned to the sea. He will merge once more into the pattern of living things—the plankton, the seals, the penguins, the whales, all the multitudinous fauna of the Antarctic Ocean.

There are no oceans here on Mars, nor have there been for at least five billion years. But there is life of some kind, down there in the badlands of Chaos II, which we never had time to explore.

Those moving patches on the orbital photographs. The evidence that whole areas of Mars have been swept clear of craters, by forces other than erosion. The long-chain, optically active carbon molecules picked up by the atmospheric samplers.

And, of course, the mystery of Viking 6. Even now, no one has been able to make any sense of those last instrument readings, before something large and heavy crushed the probe in the still, cold depths of the Martian night. . . .

And don't talk to me about *primitive* life forms in a place like this! Anything that's survived here will be so sophisticated that we may look as clumsy as dinosaurs.

There's still enough propellant in the ship's tanks to drive the Mars car clear around the planet. I have three hours of daylight left—plenty of time to get down into the valleys and well out into Chaos. After sunset, I'll still be able to make good speed with the headlights. It will be romantic, driving at night under the moons of Mars. . . .

One thing I must fix before I leave. I don't like the way Sam's lying out there. He was always so poised, so graceful. It doesn't seem right that he should look so awkward now. I must do something about it.

I wonder if *I* could have covered three hundred feet without a suit, walking slowly, steadily—the way he did, to the very end.

I must try not to look at his face.

That's it. Everything shipshape and ready to go.

The therapy has worked. I feel perfectly at ease—even contented, now that I know exactly what I'm going to do. The old nightmares have lost their power.

It is true: we all die alone. It makes no difference at the end, being fifty million miles from home.

I'm going to enjoy the drive through that lovely painted landscape. I'll be thinking of all those who dreamed about Mars—Wells and Lowell and Burroughs and Weinbaum and Bradbury. They all guessed wrong—but the reality is just as strange, just as beautiful, as they imagined.

I don't know what's waiting for me out there, and I'll probably never see it. But on this starveling world, it must be desperate for carbon, phosphorus, oxygen, calcium. It can use me.

And when my oxygen alarm gives its final "ping," somewhere down there in that haunted wilderness, I'm going to finish in style. As soon as I have difficulty in breathing, I'll get off the Mars car and start walking—with a playback unit plugged into my helmet and going full blast.

For sheer, triumphant power and glory there's nothing in the whole of music to match the Toccata and Fugue in D. I won't have time to hear all of it; that doesn't matter.

Johann Sebastian, here I come.

February 1970

A Meeting with Medusa

1. A DAY TO REMEMBER

The *Queen Elizabeth* was over three miles above the Grand Canyon, dawdling along at a comfortable hundred and eighty, when Howard Falcon spotted the camera platform closing in from the right. He had been expecting it—nothing else was cleared to fly at this altitude—but he was not too happy to have company. Although he welcomed any signs of public interest, he also wanted as much empty sky as he could get. After all, he was the first man in history to navigate a ship three-tenths of a mile long. . . .

So far, this first test flight had gone perfectly; ironically enough, the only problem had been the century-old aircraft carrier *Chairman Mao,* borrowed from the San Diego Naval Museum for support operations. Only one of *Mao*'s four nuclear reactors was still operating, and the old battle-wagon's top speed was barely thirty knots. Luckily, wind speed at sea level had been less than half this, so it had not been too difficult to maintain still air on the flight deck. Though there had been a few anxious moments during gusts, when the mooring lines had been dropped, the great dirigible had risen smoothly, straight up into the sky, as if on an invisible elevator. If all went well, *Queen Elizabeth IV* would not meet *Chairman Mao* again for another week.

Everything was under control; all test instruments gave normal readings. Commander Falcon decided to go upstairs and watch the rendezvous. He handed over to his second officer, and walked out into the transparent tubeway that led through the heart of the ship. There, as always, he was overwhelmed by the spectacle of the largest single space ever enclosed by man.

The ten spherical gas cells, each more than a hundred feet across, were ranged one behind the other like a line of gigantic soap bubbles. The tough plastic was so clear that he could see through the whole length of the array, and make out details of the elevator mechanism, more than a third of a mile from his vantage point. All around him, like a three-dimensional maze, was the structural framework of the ship—the great longitudinal girders running from nose to tail, the fifteen hoops that were the circular ribs of this sky-borne colossus, and whose varying sizes defined its graceful, streamlined profile.

At this low speed, there was little sound—merely the soft rush of wind over the envelope and an occasional creak of metal as the pattern of stresses changed. The shadowless light from the rows of lamps far overhead gave the whole scene a curiously submarine quality, and to Falcon this was enhanced by the spectacle of the translucent gasbags. He had once encountered a squadron of large but harmless jellyfish, pulsing their mindless way above a shallow tropical reef, and the plastic bubbles that gave *Queen Elizabeth* her lift often reminded him of these—especially when changing pressures made them crinkle and scatter new patterns of reflected light.

He walked down the axis of the ship until he came to the forward elevator, between gas cells one and two. Riding up to the Observation Deck, he noticed that it was uncomfortably hot, and dictated a brief memo to himself on his pocket recorder. The *Queen* obtained almost a quarter of her buoyancy from the unlimited amounts of waste heat produced by her fusion power plant. On this lightly loaded flight, indeed, only six of the ten gas cells contained helium; the remaining four were full of air. Yet she still carried two hundred tons of water as ballast. However, running the cells at high temperatures did produce problems in refrigerating the access ways; it was obvious that a little more work would have to be done there.

A refreshing blast of cooler air hit him in the face when he stepped out onto the Observation Deck and into the dazzling sunlight streaming through the plexiglass roof. Half a dozen workmen, with an equal number of superchimp assistants, were busily laying the partly completed dance floor, while others were installing electric wiring and fixing furniture. It was a scene of controlled chaos, and Falcon found it hard to believe that everything would be ready for the maiden voyage, only four weeks ahead. Well, that was not *his* problem, thank goodness. He was merely the Captain, not the Cruise Director.

The human workers waved to him, and the "simps" flashed toothy smiles, as he walked through the confusion, into the already completed Skylounge. This was his favorite place in the whole ship, and he knew that once she was operating he would never again have it all to himself. He would allow himself just five minutes of private enjoyment.

He called the bridge, checked that everything was still in order, and relaxed into one of the comfortable swivel chairs. Below, in a curve that delighted the eye, was the unbroken silver sweep of the ship's envelope. He was perched at the highest point, surveying the whole immensity of the largest vehicle ever built. And when he had tired of that—all the way out to the horizon was the fantastic wilderness carved by the Colorado River in half a billion years of time.

Apart from the camera platform (it had now fallen back and was filming from amidships), he had the sky to himself. It was blue and empty, clear down to the horizon. In his grandfather's day, Falcon knew, it would have been streaked with vapor trails and stained with smoke. Both had gone: the aerial garbage had vanished with the primitive technologies that spawned it, and the long-distance transportation of this age arced too far beyond the stratosphere for any sight or sound of it to reach Earth. Once again, the lower atmosphere belonged to the birds and the clouds—and now to *Queen Elizabeth IV*.

It was true, as the old pioneers had said at the beginning of the twentieth century: this was the only way to travel—in silence and luxury, breathing the air around you and not cut off from it, near enough to the surface to watch the ever-changing beauty of land and sea. The subsonic jets of the 1980's, packed with hundreds of passengers seated ten abreast, could not even begin to match such comfort and spaciousness.

Of course, the *Queen* would never be an economic proposition, and even if her projected sister ships were built, only a few of the world's quarter of a billion inhabitants would ever enjoy this silent gliding through the sky. But a secure and prosperous global society could afford such follies and indeed needed them for their novelty and entertainment. There were at least a million men on Earth whose discretionary income exceeded a thousand new dollars a year, so the *Queen* would not lack for passengers.

Falcon's pocket communicator beeped. The copilot was calling from the bridge.

"O.K. for rendezvous, Captain? We've got all the data we need from this run, and the TV people are getting impatient."

Falcon glanced at the camera platform, now matching his speed a tenth of a mile away.

"O.K.," he replied. "Proceed as arranged. I'll watch from here."

He walked back through the busy chaos of the Observation Deck so that he could have a better view amidships. As he did so, he could feel the change of vibration underfoot; by the time he had reached the rear of the lounge, the ship had come to rest. Using his master key, he let himself out onto the small external platform flaring from the end of the deck; half a dozen people could stand here, with only low guardrails separating them from the vast sweep of the envelope—and from the ground, thousands of feet below. It was an exciting place to be, and perfectly safe even when the ship was traveling at speed, for it was in the dead air behind the huge dorsal blister of the Observation Deck. Nevertheless, it was not intended that the passengers would have access to it; the view was a little too vertiginous.

The covers of the forward cargo hatch had already opened like giant trap doors, and the camera platform was hovering above them, preparing to descend. Along this route, in the years to come, would travel thousands of passengers and tons of supplies. Only on rare occasions would the *Queen* drop down to sea level and dock with her floating base.

A sudden gust of cross wind slapped Falcon's cheek, and he tightened his grip on the guardrail. The Grand Canyon was a bad place for turbulence, though he did not expect much at this altitude. Without any real anxiety, he focused his attention on the descending platform, now about a hundred and fifty feet above the ship. He knew that the highly skilled operator who was flying the remotely controlled vehicle had performed this simple maneuver a dozen times already; it was inconceivable that he would have any difficulties.

Yet he seemed to be reacting rather sluggishly. That last gust had drifted the platform almost to the edge of the open hatchway. Surely the pilot could have corrected before this. . . . Did he have a control problem? It was very unlikely; these remotes had multiple-redundancy, fail-safe takeovers, and any number of backup systems. Accidents were almost unheard of.

But there he went again, off to the left. Could the pilot be *drunk?* Improbable though that seemed, Falcon considered it seriously for a moment. Then he reached for his microphone switch.

Once again, without warning, he was slapped violently in the face. He hardly felt it, for he was staring in horror at the camera platform. The distant operator was fighting for control, trying to balance the craft on its jets—but he was only making matters worse. The oscillations increased—twenty degrees, forty, sixty, ninety. . . .

"Switch to automatic, you fool!" Falcon shouted uselessly into his microphone. "Your manual control's not working!"

The platform flipped over on its back. The jets no longer supported it, but drove it swiftly downward. They had suddenly become allies of the gravity they had fought until this moment.

Falcon never heard the crash, though he felt it; he was already inside the Observation Deck, racing for the elevator that would take him down to the bridge. Workmen shouted at him anxiously, asking what had happened. It would be many months before he knew the answer to that question.

Just as he was stepping into the elevator cage, he changed his mind. What if there was a power failure? Better be on the safe side, even if it took longer and time was the essence. He began to run down the spiral stairway enclosing the shaft.

Halfway down he paused for a second to inspect the damage. That damned platform had gone clear through the ship, rupturing two of the gas cells as it did so. They were still collapsing slowly, in great falling veils of plastic. He was not worried about the loss of lift—the ballast could easily take care of that, as long as eight cells remained intact. Far more serious was the possibility of structural damage. Already he could hear the great latticework around him groaning and protesting under its abnormal loads. It was not enough to have sufficient lift; unless it was properly distributed, the ship would break her back.

He was just resuming his descent when a superchimp, shrieking with fright, came racing down the elevator shaft, moving with incredible speed, hand over hand, along the *outside* of the latticework. In its terror, the poor beast had torn off its company uniform, perhaps in an unconscious attempt to regain the freedom of its ancestors.

Falcon, still descending as swiftly as he could, watched its approach with some alarm. A distraught simp was a powerful and potentially dangerous animal, especially if fear overcame its conditioning. As it overtook him, it started to call out a string of words, but they were all jumbled together, and the only one he could recognize was a plaintive, frequently repeated "boss." Even now, Falcon realized, it looked toward humans for guidance. He felt sorry for the creature, involved in a man-made disaster beyond its comprehension, and for which it bore no responsibility.

It stopped opposite him, on the other side of the lattice; there was nothing to prevent it from coming through the open framework if it wished. Now its face was only inches from his, and he was looking straight into the terrified eyes. Never before had he been so close to a simp, and able to study its features in such detail. He felt that strange mingling of kinship and discomfort that all men experience when they gaze thus into the mirror of time.

His presence seemed to have calmed the creature. Falcon pointed up the shaft, back toward the Observation Deck, and said very clearly and precisely: "Boss—boss—*go*." To his relief, the simp understood; it gave him a grimace that might have been a smile, and at once started to race back the way it had come. Falcon had given it the best advice he could. If any safety remained aboard the *Queen,* it was in that direction. But his duty lay in the other.

He had almost completed his descent when, with a sound of rending metal, the vessel pitched nose down, and the lights went out. But he could still see quite well, for a shaft of sunlight streamed through the open hatch and the huge tear in the envelope. Many years ago he had stood in a great cathedral nave watching the light pouring through the stained-glass windows and forming pools of multicolored radiance on the ancient flagstones. The dazzling shaft of sunlight through the ruined fabric high above reminded him of that moment. He was in a cathedral of metal, falling down the sky.

When he reached the bridge, and was able for the first time to look outside, he was horrified to see how close the ship was to the ground. Only three thousand feet below were the beautiful and deadly pinnacles of rock and the red rivers of mud that were still carving their way down into the past. There was no level area anywhere in sight where a ship as large as the *Queen* could come to rest on an even keel.

A glance at the display board told him that all the ballast had gone. However, rate of descent had been reduced to a few yards a second; they still had a fighting chance.

Without a word, Falcon eased himself into the pilot's seat and took over such control as still remained. The instrument board showed him everything he wished to know; speech was superfluous. In the background, he could hear the Communications Officer giving a running report over the radio. By this time, all the news channels of Earth would have been pre-empted, and he could imagine the utter frustration of the program controllers. One of the most spectacular wrecks in history was occurring—without a single camera to record it. The last moments of the *Queen* would never fill millions with awe and terror, as had those of the *Hindenburg*, a century and a half before.

Now the ground was only about seventeen hundred feet away, still coming up slowly. Though he had full thrust, he had not dared to use it, lest the weakened structure collapse; but now he realized that he had no choice. The wind was taking them toward a fork in the canyon, where the river was split by a wedge of rock like the prow of some gigantic, fossilized ship of stone. If she continued on her present course, the *Queen* would straddle that triangular plateau and come to rest with at least a third of her length jutting out over nothingness; she would snap like a rotten stick.

Far away, above the sound of straining metal and escaping gas, came the familiar whistle of the jets as Falcon opened up the lateral thrusters. The ship staggered, and began to slew to port. The shriek of tearing metal was now almost continuous—and the rate of descent had started to increase ominously. A glance at the damage-control board showed that cell number five had just gone.

The ground was only yards away. Even now, he could not tell whether his maneuver would succeed or fail. He switched the thrust vectors over to vertical, giving maximum lift to reduce the force of impact.

The crash seemed to last forever. It was not violent—merely prolonged, and irresistible. It seemed that the whole universe was falling about them.

The sound of crunching metal came nearer, as if some great beast were eating its way through the dying ship.

Then floor and ceiling closed upon him like a vice.

2. "BECAUSE IT'S THERE"

"Why do you want to go to Jupiter?"

"As Springer said when he lifted for Pluto—'because it's there.' "

"Thanks. Now we've got *that* out of the way—the real reason."

Howard Falcon smiled, though only those who knew him well could have interpreted the slight, leathery grimace. Webster was one of them; for more than twenty years they had been involved in each other's projects. They had shared triumphs and disasters—including the greatest disaster of all.

"Well, Springer's cliché is still valid. We've landed on all the terrestrial planets, but none of the gas giants. They are the only real challenge left in the solar system."

"An expensive one. Have you worked out the cost?"

"As well as I can; here are the estimates. Remember, though—this isn't a one-shot mission, but a transportation system. Once it's proved out, it can be used over and over again. And it will open up not merely Jupiter, but *all* the giants."

Webster looked at the figures, and whistled.

"Why not start with an easier planet—Uranus, for example? Half the gravity, and less than half the escape velocity. Quieter weather, too—if that's the right word for it."

Webster had certainly done his homework. But that, of course, was why he was head of Long-Range Planning.

"There's very little saving—when you allow for the extra distance and the logistics problems. For Jupiter, we can use the facilities of Ganymede. Beyond Saturn, we'd have to establish a new supply base."

Logical, thought Webster; but he was sure that it was not the important reason. Jupiter was lord of the solar system; Falcon would be interested in no lesser challenge.

"Besides," Falcon continued, "Jupiter is a major scientific scandal. It's more than a hundred years since its radio storms were discovered, but we still don't know what causes them—and the Great Red Spot is as big a mystery as ever. That's why I can get matching funds from the Bureau of Astronautics. Do you know how many probes they have dropped into that atmosphere?"

"A couple of hundred, I believe."

"*Three* hundred and twenty-six, over the last fifty years—about a quarter of them total failures. Of course, they've learned a hell of a lot, but they've barely scratched the planet. Do you realize how *big* it is?"

"More than ten times the size of Earth."

"Yes, yes—but do you know what that really means?"

Falcon pointed to the large globe in the corner of Webster's office.

"Look at India—how small it seems. Well, if you skinned Earth and spread it out on the surface of Jupiter, it would look about as big as India does here."

There was a long silence while Webster contemplated the equation: Jupiter is to Earth as Earth is to India. Falcon had—deliberately, of course—chosen the best possible example. . . .

Was it already ten years ago? Yes, it must have been. The crash lay seven years in the past (*that* date was engraved on his heart), and those initial tests had taken place three years before the first and last flight of the *Queen Elizabeth*.

Ten years ago, then, Commander (no, Lieutenant) Falcon had invited him to a preview—a three-day drift across the northern plains of India, within sight of the Himalayas. "Perfectly safe," he had promised. "It will get you away from the office—and will teach you what this whole thing is about."

Webster had not been disappointed. Next to his first journey to the Moon, it had been the most memorable experience of his life. And yet, as Falcon had assured him, it had been perfectly safe, and quite uneventful.

They had taken off from Srinagar just before dawn, with the huge silver bubble of the balloon already catching the first light of the Sun. The ascent had been made in total silence; there were none of the roaring propane burners that had lifted the hot-air balloons of an earlier age. All the heat they needed came from the little pulsed-fusion reactor, weighing only about two hundred and twenty pounds, hanging in the open mouth of the envelope. While they were climbing, its laser was zapping ten times a second, igniting the merest whiff of deuterium fuel. Once they had reached altitude, it would fire only a few times a minute, making up for the heat lost through the great gasbag overhead.

And so, even while they were almost a mile above the ground, they could hear dogs barking, people shouting, bells ringing. Slowly the vast, Sun-smitten landscape expanded around them. Two hours later, they had leveled out at three miles and were taking frequent draughts of oxygen. They could relax and admire the scenery; the on-board instrumentation was doing all the work—gathering the information that would be required by the designers of the still-unnamed liner of the skies.

It was a perfect day. The southwest monsoon would not break for another month, and there was hardly a cloud in the sky. Time seemed to have come to a stop; they resented the hourly radio reports which interrupted their reverie. And all around, to the horizon and far beyond, was that infinite, ancient landscape, drenched with history—a patchwork of villages, fields, temples, lakes, irrigation canals. . . .

With a real effort, Webster broke the hypnotic spell of that ten-year-old memory. It had converted him to lighter-than-air flight—and it had made him realize the enormous size of India, even in a world that could be circled within ninety minutes. And yet, he repeated to himself, Jupiter is to Earth as Earth is to India. . . .

"Granted your argument," he said, "and supposing the funds are available, there's another question you have to answer. Why should you do better than the—what is it—three hundred and twenty-six robot probes that have already made the trip?"

"I am better qualified than they were—as an observer, and as a pilot. *Especially* as a pilot. Don't forget—I've more experience of lighter-than-air flight than anyone in the world."

"You could still serve as controller, and sit safely on Ganymede."

"*But that's just the point!* They've already done that. Don't you remember what killed the *Queen?*"

Webster knew perfectly well; but he merely answered: "Go on."

"*Time lag—time lag!* That idiot of a platform controller thought he was using a local radio circuit. But he'd been accidentally switched through a satellite—oh, maybe it wasn't his fault, but he should have noticed. That's a half-second time lag for the round trip. Even then it wouldn't have mattered flying in calm air. It was the turbulence over the Grand Canyon that did it. When the platform tipped, and he corrected for that—it had already tipped the other way. Ever tried to drive a car over a bumpy road with a half-second delay in the steering?"

"No, and I don't intend to try. But I can imagine it."

"Well, Ganymede is a million kilometers from Jupiter. That means a round-trip delay of six seconds. No, you need a controller on the spot—to handle emergencies in real time. Let me show you something. Mind if I use this?"

"Go ahead."

Falcon picked up a postcard that was lying on Webster's desk; they were almost obsolete on Earth, but this one showed a 3-D view of a Martian landscape, and was decorated with exotic and expensive stamps. He held it so that it dangled vertically.

"This is an old trick, but helps to make my point. Place your thumb and finger on either side, not quite touching. That's right."

Webster put out his hand, almost but not quite gripping the card.

"Now catch it."

Falcon waited for a few seconds; then, without warning, he let go of the card. Webster's thumb and finger closed on empty air.

"I'll do it again, just to show there's no deception. You see?"

Once again, the falling card had slipped through Webster's fingers.

"Now you try it on me."

This time, Webster grasped the card and dropped it without warning. It had scarcely moved before Falcon had caught it. Webster almost imagined he could hear a click, so swift was the other's reaction.

"When they put me together again," Falcon remarked in an expressionless voice, "the surgeons made some improvements. This is one of them—and there are others. I want to make the most of them. Jupiter is the place where I can do it."

Webster stared for long seconds at the fallen card, absorbing the improbable colors of the Trivium Charontis Escarpment. Then he said quietly: "I understand. How long do you think it will take?"

"With your help, plus the Bureau, plus all the science foundations we can drag in—oh, three years. Then a year for trials—we'll have to send in at least two test models. So, with luck—five years."

"That's about what I thought. I hope you get your luck; you've earned it. But there's one thing I won't do."

"What's that?"

"Next time you go ballooning, don't expect *me* as passenger."

3. THE WORLD OF THE GODS

The fall from Jupiter V to Jupiter itself takes only three and a half hours. Few men could have slept on so awesome a journey. Sleep was a weakness that Howard Falcon hated, and the little he still required brought dreams that time had not yet been able to exorcise. But he could expect no rest in the three days that lay ahead, and must seize what he could during the long fall down into that ocean of clouds, some sixty thousand miles below.

As soon as *Kon-Tiki* had entered her transfer orbit and all the computer checks were satisfactory, he prepared for the last sleep he might ever know. It seemed appropriate that at almost the same moment Jupiter eclipsed the bright and tiny Sun as he swept into the monstrous shadow of the planet. For a few minutes a strange golden twilight enveloped the ship; then a quarter of the sky became an utterly black hole in space, while the rest was a blaze of stars. No matter how far one traveled across the solar system, *they* never changed; these same constellations now shone on Earth, millions of miles away. The only novelties here were the small, pale crescents of Callisto and Ganymede; doubtless there were a dozen other moons up there in the sky, but they were all much too tiny, and too distant, for the unaided eye to pick them out.

"Closing down for two hours," he reported to the mother ship, hanging almost a thousand miles above the desolate rocks of Jupiter V, in the radiation shadow of the tiny satellite. If it never served any other useful purpose, Jupiter V was a cosmic bulldozer perpetually sweeping up the charged particles that made it unhealthy to linger close to Jupiter. Its wake was almost free of radiation, and there a ship could park in perfect safety, while death sleeted invisibly all around.

Falcon switched on the sleep inducer, and consciousness faded swiftly out as the electric pulses surged gently through his brain. While *Kon-Tiki* fell toward Jupiter, gaining speed second by second in that enormous gravitational field, he slept without dreams. They always came when he awoke; and he had brought his nightmares with him from Earth.

Yet he never dreamed of the crash itself, though he often found himself again face to face with that terrified superchimp, as he descended the spiral stairway between the collapsing gasbags. None of the simps had survived; those that were not killed outright were so badly injured that they had been painlessly "euthed." He sometimes wondered why he dreamed only of this doomed creature—which he had never met before the last minutes of its life—and not of the friends and colleagues he had lost aboard the dying *Queen*.

The dreams he feared most always began with his first return to consciousness. There had been little physical pain; in fact, there had been no sensation of any kind. He was in darkness and silence, and did not even seem to be breathing. And—strangest of all—he could not locate his limbs. He could move neither his hands nor his feet, because he did not know where they were.

The silence had been the first to yield. After hours, or days, he had become aware of a faint throbbing, and eventually, after long thought, he deduced that this was the beating of his own heart. That was the first of his many mistakes.

Then there had been faint pinpricks, sparkles of light, ghosts of pressures upon still-unresponsive limbs. One by one his senses had returned, and pain had come with them. He had had to learn everything anew, recapitulating infancy and babyhood. Though his memory was unaffected, and he could understand words that were spoken to him, it was months before he was able to answer except by the flicker of an eyelid. He could remember the moments of triumph when he had spoken the first word, turned the page of a book—and, finally, learned to move under his own power. *That* was a victory indeed, and it had taken him almost two years to prepare for it. A hundred times he had envied that dead superchimp, but *he* had been given no choice. The doctors had made their decision—and now, twelve years later, he was where no human being had ever traveled before, and moving faster than any man in history.

Kon-Tiki was just emerging from shadow, and the Jovian dawn bridged the sky ahead in a titanic bow of light, when the persistent buzz of the alarm dragged Falcon up from sleep. The inevitable nightmares (he had been trying to summon a nurse, but did not even have the strength to push the button) swiftly faded from consciousness. The greatest—and perhaps last—adventure of his life was before him.

He called Mission Control, now almost sixty thousand miles away and falling swiftly below the curve of Jupiter, to report that everything was in order. His velocity had just passed thirty-one miles a second (*that* was one for the books) and in half an hour *Kon-Tiki* would hit the outer fringes of the atmosphere, as he started on the most difficult re-entry in the entire solar system. Although scores of probes had survived this flaming ordeal, they had been tough, solidly packed masses of instrumentation, able to withstand several hundred gravities of drag. *Kon-Tiki* would hit peaks of thirty g's, and would average more than ten, before she came to rest in the upper reaches of the Jovian atmosphere. Very carefully and thoroughly, Falcon began to attach the elaborate system of restraints that would anchor him to the walls of the cabin. When he had finished, he was virtually a part of the ship's structure.

The clock was counting backward; one hundred seconds to re-entry. For better or worse, he was committed. In a minute and a half, he would graze the Jovian atmosphere, and would be caught irrevocably in the grip of the giant.

The countdown was three seconds late—not at all bad, considering the unknowns involved. From beyond the walls of the capsule came a ghostly sighing, which rose steadily to a high-pitched, screaming roar. The noise was quite different from that of a re-entry on Earth or Mars; in this thin atmosphere of hydrogen and helium, all sounds were transformed a couple of octaves upward. On Jupiter, even thunder would have falsetto overtones.

With the rising scream came mounting weight; within seconds, he was completely immobilized. His field of vision contracted until it embraced only the clock and the accelerometer; fifteen g, and four hundred and eighty seconds to go. . . .

He never lost consciousness; but then, he had not expected to. *Kon-Tiki*'s trail through the Jovian atmosphere must be really spectacular—by this time, thousands of miles long. Five hundred seconds after entry, the drag began to taper off: ten g, five g, two. . . . Then weight vanished almost completely. He was falling free, all his enormous orbital velocity destroyed.

There was a sudden jolt as the incandescent remnants of the heat shield were jettisoned. It had done its work and would not be needed again; Jupiter could have it now. He released all but two of the restraining buckles, and waited for the automatic sequencer to start the next, and most critical, series of events.

He did not see the first drogue parachute pop out, but he could feel the slight jerk, and the rate of fall diminished immediately. *Kon-Tiki* had lost all her horizontal speed and was going straight down at almost a thousand miles an hour.

Everything depended on what happened in the next sixty seconds.

There went the second drogue. He looked up through the overhead window and saw, to his immense relief, that clouds of glittering foil were billowing out behind the falling ship. Like a great flower unfurling, the thousands of cubic yards of the balloon spread out across the sky, scooping up the thin gas until it was fully inflated. *Kon-Tiki*'s rate of fall dropped to a few miles an hour and remained constant. Now there was plenty of time; it would take him days to fall all the way down to the surface of Jupiter.

But he would get there eventually, even if he did nothing about it. The balloon overhead was merely acting as an efficient parachute. It was providing no lift; nor could it do so, while the gas inside and out was the same.

With its characteristic and rather disconcerting crack the fusion reactor started up, pouring torrents of heat into the envelope overhead. Within five minutes, the rate of fall had become zero; within six, the ship had started to rise. According to the radar altimeter, it had leveled out at about two hundred and sixty-seven miles above the surface—or whatever passed for a surface on Jupiter.

Only one kind of balloon will work in an atmosphere of hydrogen, which is the lightest of all gases—and that is a hot-hydrogen balloon. As long as the fuser kept ticking over, Falcon could remain aloft, drifting across a world that could hold a hundred Pacifics. After traveling over three hundred million miles, *Kon-Tiki* had at last begun to justify her name. She was an aerial raft, adrift upon the currents of the Jovian atmosphere.

Though a whole new world was lying around him, it was more than an hour before Falcon could examine the view. First he had to check all the capsule's systems and test its response to the controls. He had to learn how much extra heat was necessary to produce a desired rate of ascent, and how much gas he must vent in order to descend. Above all, there was the question of stability. He must adjust the length of the cables attaching his capsule to the huge, pear-shaped balloon, to damp out vibrations and get the smoothest possible ride. Thus far, he was lucky; at this level, the wind was steady, and the Doppler reading on the invisible surface gave him a ground speed of two hundred seventeen and a half miles an hour. For Jupiter, that was modest; winds of up to a thousand had been observed. But mere speed was, of course, unimportant; the real danger was turbulence. If he ran into that, only skill and experience and swift reaction could save him—and these were not matters that could yet be programed into a computer.

Not until he was satisfied that he had got the feel of his strange craft did Falcon pay any attention to Mission Control's pleadings. Then he deployed the booms carrying the instrumentation and the atmospheric samplers. The capsule now resembled a rather untidy Christmas tree, but still rode smoothly down the Jovian winds while it radioed its torrents of information to the recorders on the ship miles above. And now, at last, he could look around. . . .

His first impression was unexpected, and even a little disappointing. As far as the scale of things was concerned, he might have been ballooning over an ordinary cloudscape on Earth. The horizon seemed at a normal distance; there was no feeling at all that he was on a world eleven times the diameter of his own. Then he looked at the infrared radar, sounding the layers of atmosphere beneath him—and knew how badly his eyes had been deceived.

That layer of clouds apparently about three miles away was really more than thirty-seven miles below. And the horizon, whose distance he would have guessed at about one hundred and twenty-five, was actually eighteen hundred miles from the ship.

The crystalline clarity of the hydrohelium atmosphere and the enormous curvature of the planet had fooled him completely. It was even harder to judge distances here than on the Moon; everything he saw must be multiplied by at least ten.

It was a simple matter, and he should have been prepared for it. Yet somehow, it disturbed him profoundly. He did not feel that Jupiter was huge, but that *he* had shrunk—to a tenth of his normal size. Perhaps, with time, he would grow accustomed to the inhuman scale of this world; yet as he stared toward that unbelievably distant horizon, he felt as if a wind colder than the atmosphere around him was blowing through his soul. Despite all his arguments, this might never be a place for man. He could well be both the first and the last to descend through the clouds of Jupiter.

The sky above was almost black, except for a few wisps of ammonia cirrus perhaps twelve miles overhead. It was cold up there, on the fringes of space, but both pressure and temperature increased rapidly with depth. At the level where *Kon-Tiki* was drifting now, it was fifty below zero, and the pressure was five atmospheres. Sixty-five miles farther down, it would be as warm as equatorial Earth, and the pressure about the same as at the bottom of one of the shallower seas. Ideal conditions for life. . . .

A quarter of the brief Jovian day had already gone; the sun was halfway up the sky, but the light on the unbroken cloudscape below had a curious mellow quality. That extra three hundred million miles had robbed the Sun of all its power. Though the sky was clear, Falcon found himself continually thinking that it was a heavily overcast day. When night fell, the onset of darkness would be swift indeed; though it was still morning, there was a sense of autumnal twilight in the air. But autumn, of course, was something that never came to Jupiter. There were no seasons here.

Kon-Tiki had come down in the exact center of the equatorial zone—the least colorful part of the planet. The sea of clouds that stretched out to the horizon was tinted a pale salmon; there were none of the yellows and pinks and even reds that banded Jupiter at higher altitudes. The Great Red Spot itself—most spectacular of all of the planet's features—lay thousands of miles to the south. It had been a temptation to descend there, but the south tropical disturbance was unusually active, with currents reaching over nine hundred miles an hour. It would have been asking for trouble to head into that maelstrom of unknown forces. The Great Red Spot and its mysteries would have to wait for future expeditions.

The Sun, moving across the sky twice as swiftly as it did on Earth, was now nearing the zenith and had become eclipsed by the great silver canopy of the balloon. *Kon-Tiki* was still drifting swiftly and smoothly westward at a steady two hundred and seventeen and a half, but only the radar gave any indication of this. Was it always as calm here? Falcon asked himself. The scientists who had talked learnedly of the Jovian doldrums, and had predicted that the equator would be the quietest place, seemed to know what they were talking about, after all. He had been profoundly skeptical of all such forecasts, and had agreed with one unusually modest researcher who had told him bluntly: "There are *no* experts on Jupiter." Well, there would be at least one by the end of this day.

If he managed to survive until then.

4. THE VOICES OF THE DEEP

That first day, the Father of the Gods smiled upon him. It was as calm and peaceful here on Jupiter as it had been, years ago, when he was drifting with Webster across the plains of northern India. Falcon had time to master his new skills, until *Kon-Tiki* seemed an extension of his own body. Such luck was more than he had dared to hope for, and he began to wonder what price he might have to pay for it.

The five hours of daylight were almost over; the clouds below were full of shadows, which gave them a massive solidity they had not possessed when the Sun was higher. Color was swiftly draining from the sky, except in the west itself, where a band of deepening purple lay along the horizon. Above this band was the thin crescent of a closer moon, pale and bleached against the utter blackness beyond.

With a speed perceptible to the eye, the Sun went straight down over the edge of Jupiter, over eighteen hundred miles away. The stars came out in their legions—and there was the beautiful evening star of Earth, on the very frontier of twilight, reminding him how far he was from home. It followed the Sun down into the west. Man's first night on Jupiter had begun.

With the onset of darkness, *Kon-Tiki* started to sink. The balloon was no longer heated by the feeble sunlight and was losing a small part of its buoyancy. Falcon did nothing to increase lift; he had expected this and was planning to descend.

The invisible cloud deck was still over thirty miles below, and he would reach it about midnight. It showed up clearly on the infrared radar, which also reported that it contained a vast array of complex carbon compounds, as well as the usual hydrogen, helium, and ammonia. The chemists were dying for samples of that fluffy, pinkish stuff; though some atmospheric probes had already gathered a few grams, that had only whetted their appetites. Half the basic molecules of life were here, floating high above the surface of Jupiter. And where there was food, could life be far away? That was the question that, after more than a hundred years, no one had been able to answer.

The infrared was blocked by the clouds, but the microwave radar sliced right through and showed layer after layer, all the way down to the hidden surface almost two hundred and fifty miles below. That was barred to him by enormous pressures and temperatures; not even robot probes had ever reached it intact. It lay in tantalizing inaccessibility at the bottom of the radar screen, slightly fuzzy, and showing a curious granular structure that his equipment could not resolve.

An hour after sunset, he dropped his first probe. It fell swiftly for about sixty miles, then began to float in the denser atmosphere, sending back torrents of radio signals, which he relayed to Mission Control. Then there was nothing else to do until sunrise, except to keep an eye on the rate of descent, monitor the instruments, and answer occasional queries. While she was drifting in this steady current, *Kon-Tiki* could look after herself.

Just before midnight, a woman controller came on watch and introduced herself with the usual pleasantries. Ten minutes later she called again, her voice at once serious and excited.

"Howard! Listen in on channel forty-six—high gain."

Channel forty-six? There were so many telemetering circuits that he knew the numbers of only those that were critical; but as soon as he threw the switch, he recognized this one. He was plugged in to the microphone on the probe, floating more than eighty miles below him in an atmosphere now almost as dense as water.

At first, there was only a soft hiss of whatever strange winds stirred down in the darkness of that unimaginable world. And then, out of the background noise, there slowly emerged a booming vibration that grew louder and louder, like the beating of a gigantic drum. It was so low that it was felt as much as heard, and the beats steadily increased their tempo, though the pitch never changed. Now it was a swift, almost infrasonic throbbing. Then, suddenly, in mid-vibration, it stopped—so abruptly that the mind could not accept the silence, but memory continued to manufacture a ghostly echo in the deepest caverns of the brain.

It was the most extraordinary sound that Falcon had ever heard, even among the multitudinous noises of Earth. He could think of no natural phenomenon that could have caused it; nor was it like the cry of any animal, not even one of the great whales. . . .

It came again, following exactly the same pattern. Now that he was prepared for it, he estimated the length of the sequence; from first faint throb to final crescendo, it lasted just over ten seconds.

And this time there was a real echo, very faint and far away. Perhaps it came from one of the many reflecting layers, deeper in this stratified atmosphere; perhaps it was another, more distant source. Falcon waited for a second echo, but it never came.

Mission Control reacted quickly and asked him to drop another probe at once. With two microphones operating, it would be possible to find the approximate location of the sources. Oddly enough, none of *Kon-Tiki*'s own external mikes could detect anything except wind noises. The boomings, whatever they were, must have been trapped and channeled beneath an atmospheric reflecting layer far below.

They were coming, it was soon discovered, from a cluster of sources about twelve hundred miles away. The distance gave no indication of their power; in Earth's oceans, quite feeble sounds could travel equally far. And as for the obvious assumption that living creatures were responsible, the Chief Exobiologist quickly ruled that out.

"I'll be very disappointed," said Dr. Brenner, "if there are no microorganisms or plants there. But nothing like animals, because there's no free oxygen. All biochemical reactions on Jupiter must be low-energy ones—there's just no way an active creature could generate enough power to function."

Falcon wondered if this was true; he had heard the argument before, and reserved judgment.

"In any case," continued Brenner, "some of those sound waves are a hundred yards long! Even an animal as big as a whale couldn't produce them. They *must* have a natural origin."

Yes, that seemed plausible, and probably the physicists would be able to come up with an explanation. What would a blind alien make, Falcon wondered, of the sounds he might hear when standing beside a stormy sea, or a geyser, or a volcano, or a waterfall? He might well attribute them to some huge beast.

About an hour before sunrise the voices of the deep died away, and Falcon began to busy himself with preparation for the dawn of his second day. *Kon-Tiki* was now only three miles above the nearest cloud layer; the external pressure had risen to ten atmospheres, and the temperature was a tropical thirty degrees. A man could be comfortable here with no more equipment than a breathing mask and the right grade of heliox mixture.

"We've some good news for you," Mission Control reported,

soon after dawn. "The cloud layer's breaking up. You'll have partial clearing in an hour—but watch out for turbulence."

"I've already noticed some," Falcon answered. "How far down will I be able to see?"

"At least twelve miles, down to the second thermocline. *That* cloud deck is solid—it never breaks."

And it's out of my reach, Falcon told himself; the temperature down there must be over a hundred degrees. This was the first time that any balloonist had ever had to worry, not about his ceiling, but about his basement!

Ten minutes later he could see what Mission Control had already observed from its superior vantage point. There was a change in color near the horizon, and the cloud layer had become ragged and humpy, as if something had torn it open. He turned up his little nuclear furnace and gave *Kon-Tiki* another three miles of altitude, so that he could get a better view.

The sky below was clearing rapidly, completely, as if something was dissolving the solid overcast. An abyss was opening before his eyes. A moment later he sailed out over the edge of a cloud canyon about twelve miles deep and six hundred miles wide.

A new world lay spread beneath him; Jupiter had stripped away one of its many veils. The second layer of clouds, unattainably far below, was much darker in color than the first. It was almost salmon pink, and curiously mottled with little islands of brick red. They were all oval-shaped, with their long axes pointing east-west, in the direction of the prevailing wind. There were hundreds of them, all about the same size, and they reminded Falcon of puffy little cumulus clouds in the terrestrial sky.

He reduced buoyancy, and *Kon-Tiki* began to drop down the face of the dissolving cliff. It was then that he noticed the snow.

White flakes were forming in the air and drifting slowly downward. Yet it was much too warm for snow—and, in any event, there was scarcely a trace of water at this altitude.

Moreover, there was no glitter or sparkle about these flakes as they went cascading down into the depths. When, presently, a few landed on an instrument boom outside the main viewing port, he saw that they were a dull, opaque white—not crystalline at all—and quite large—several inches across. They looked like wax, and Falcon guessed that this was precisely what they were. Some chemical reaction was taking place in the atmosphere around him, condensing out the hydrocarbons floating in the Jovian air.

About sixty miles ahead, a disturbance was taking place in the cloud layer. The little red ovals were being jostled around, and were beginning to form a spiral—the familiar cyclonic pattern so common in the meteorology of Earth. The vortex was emerging with astonishing speed; if that was a storm ahead, Falcon told himself, he was in big trouble.

And then his concern changed to wonder—and to fear. What was developing in his line of flight was not a storm at all. Something enormous—something scores of miles across—was rising through the clouds.

The reassuring thought that it, too, might be a cloud—a thunderhead boiling up from the lower levels of the atmosphere—lasted only a few seconds. No; this was *solid.* It shouldered its way through the pink-and-salmon overcast like an iceberg rising from the deeps.

An *iceberg* floating on hydrogen? That was impossible, of course; but perhaps it was not too remote an analogy. As soon as he focused the telescope upon the enigma, Falcon saw that it was a whitish, crystalline mass, threaded with streaks of red and brown. It must be, he decided, the same stuff as the "snowflakes" falling around him—a mountain range of wax. And it was not, he soon realized, as solid as he had thought; around the edges it was continually crumbling and re-forming. . . .

"I know what it is," he radioed Mission Control, which for the last few minutes had been asking anxious questions. "It's a mass of bubbles—some kind of foam. Hydrocarbon froth. Get the chemists working on . . . *Just a minute!*"

"What is it?" called Mission Control. "What is it?"

He ignored the frantic pleas from space and concentrated all his mind upon the image in the telescope field. He had to be sure; if he made a mistake, he would be the laughingstock of the solar system.

Then he relaxed, glanced at the clock, and switched off the nagging voice from Jupiter V.

"Hello, Mission Control," he said, very formally. "This is Howard Falcon aboard *Kon-Tiki.* Ephemeris Time nineteen hours twenty-one minutes fifteen seconds. Latitude zero degrees five minutes North. Longitude one hundred five degrees forty-two minutes, System One.

"Tell Dr. Brenner that there is life on Jupiter. And it's *big. . . .*"

5. THE WHEELS OF POSEIDON

"I'm very happy to be proved wrong," Dr. Brenner radioed back cheerfully. "Nature always has something up her sleeve. Keep the long-focus camera on target and give us the steadiest pictures you can."

The things moving up and down those waxen slopes were still too far away for Falcon to make out many details, and they must have been very large to be visible at all at such a distance. Almost black, and shaped like arrowheads, they maneuvered by slow undulations of their entire bodies, so that they looked rather like giant manta rays, swimming above some tropical reef.

Perhaps they were sky-borne cattle, browsing on the cloud pastures of Jupiter, for they seemed to be feeding along the dark, red-brown streaks that ran like dried-up river beds down the flanks of the floating cliffs. Occasionally, one of them would dive headlong into the mountain of foam and disappear completely from sight.

Kon-Tiki was moving only slowly with respect to the cloud layer below; it would be at least three hours before she was above those ephemeral hills. She was in a race with the Sun.

Falcon hoped that darkness would not fall before he could get a good view of the mantas, as he had christened them, as well as the fragile landscape over which they flapped their way.

It was a long three hours. During the whole time, he kept the external microphones on full gain, wondering if here was the source of that booming in the night. The mantas were certainly large enough to have produced it; when he could get an accurate measurement, he discovered that they were almost a hundred yards across the wings. That was three times the length of the largest whale—though he doubted if they could weigh more than a few tons.

Half an hour before sunset, *Kon-Tiki* was almost above the "mountains."

"No," said Falcon, answering Mission Control's repeated questions about the mantas, "they're still showing no reaction to me. I don't think they're intelligent—they look like harmless vegetarians. And even if they try to chase me, I'm sure they can't reach my altitude."

Yet he was a little disappointed when the mantas showed not the slightest interest in him as he sailed high above their feeding ground. Perhaps they had no way of detecting his presence. When he examined and photographed them through the telescope, he could see no signs of any sense organs. The creatures were simply huge black deltas, rippling over hills and valleys that, in reality, were little more substantial than the clouds of Earth. Though they looked solid, Falcon knew that anyone who stepped on those white mountains would go crashing through them as if they were made of tissue paper.

At close quarters he could see the myriads of cellules or bubbles from which they were formed. Some of these were quite large—a yard or so in diameter—and Falcon wondered in what witches' cauldron of hydrocarbons they had been brewed. There must be enough petrochemicals deep down in the atmosphere of Jupiter to supply all Earth's needs for a million years.

The short day had almost gone when he passed over the crest of the waxen hills, and the light was fading rapidly along their lower slopes. There were no mantas on this western side, and for some reason the topography was very different. The foam was sculptured into long, level terraces, like the interior of a lunar crater. He could almost imagine that they were gigantic steps leading down to the hidden surface of the planet.

And on the lowest of those steps, just clear of the swirling clouds that the mountain had displaced when it came surging skyward, was a roughly oval mass, one or two miles across. It was difficult to see, since it was only a little darker than the gray-white foam on which it rested. Falcon's first thought was that he was looking at a forest of pallid trees, like giant mushrooms that had never seen the Sun.

Yes, it must be a forest—he could see hundreds of thin trunks, springing from the white waxy froth in which they were rooted. But the trees were packed astonishingly close together; there was scarcely any space between them. Perhaps it was not a forest, after all, but a single enormous tree—like one of the giant multi-trunked banyans of the East. Once he had seen a banyan tree in Java that was over six hundred and fifty yards across; this monster was at least ten times that size.

The light had almost gone. The cloudscape had turned purple with refracted sunlight, and in a few seconds that, too, would have vanished. In the last light of his second day on Jupiter, Howard Falcon saw—or thought he saw—something that cast the gravest doubts on his interpretation of the white oval.

Unless the dim light had totally deceived him, those hundreds of thin trunks were beating back and forth, in perfect synchronism, like fronds of kelp rocking in the surge.

And the tree was no longer in the place where he had first seen it.

"Sorry about this," said Mission Control, soon after sunset, "but we think Source Beta is going to blow within the next hour. Probability seventy per cent."

Falcon glanced quickly at the chart. Beta—Jupiter latitude

one hundred and forty degrees—was over eighteen thousand six hundred miles away and well below his horizon. Even though major eruptions ran as high as ten megatons, he was much too far away for the shock wave to be a serious danger. The radio storm that it would trigger was, however, quite a different matter.

The decameter outbursts that sometimes made Jupiter the most powerful radio source in the whole sky had been discovered back in the 1950's, to the utter astonishment of the astronomers. Now, more than a century later, their real cause was still a mystery. Only the symptoms were understood; the explanation was completely unknown.

The "volcano" theory had best stood the test of time, although no one imagined that this word had the same meaning on Jupiter as on Earth. At frequent intervals—often several times a day—titanic eruptions occurred in the lower depths of the atmosphere, probably on the hidden surface of the planet itself. A great column of gas, more than six hundred miles high, would start boiling upward as if determined to escape into space.

Against the most powerful gravitational field of all the planets, it had no chance. Yet some traces—a mere few million tons—usually managed to reach the Jovian ionosphere; and when they did, all hell broke loose.

The radiation belts surrounding Jupiter completely dwarf the feeble Van Allen belts of Earth. When they are short-circuited by an ascending column of gas, the result is an electrical discharge millions of times more powerful than any terrestrial flash of lightning; it sends a colossal thunderclap of radio noise flooding across the entire solar system and on out to the stars.

It had been discovered that these radio outbursts came from four main areas of the planet. Perhaps there were weaknesses there that allowed the fires of the interior to break out from time to time. The scientists on Ganymede, largest of Jupiter's many moons, now thought that they could predict the onset of a decameter storm; their accuracy was about as good as a weather forecaster's of the early 1900's.

Falcon did not know whether to welcome or to fear a radio storm; it would certainly add to the value of the mission—if he survived it. His course had been planned to keep as far as possible from the main centers of disturbance, especially the most active one, Source Alpha. As luck would have it, the threatening Beta was the closest to him. He hoped that the distance, almost three-fourths the circumference of Earth, was safe enough.

"Probability ninety per cent," said Mission Control with a distinct note of urgency. "And forget that hour. Ganymede says it may be any moment."

The radio had scarcely fallen silent when the reading on the magnetic field-strength meter started to shoot upward. Before it could go off scale, it reversed and began to drop as rapidly as it had risen. Far away and thousands of miles below, something had given the planet's molten core a titanic jolt.

"There she blows!" called Mission Control.

"Thanks, I already know. When will the storm hit me?"

"You can expect onset in five minutes. Peak in ten."

Far around the curve of Jupiter, a funnel of gas as wide as the Pacific Ocean was climbing spaceward at thousands of miles an hour. Already, the thunderstorms of the lower atmosphere would be raging around it—but they were nothing compared with the fury that would explode when the radiation belt was reached and began dumping its surplus electrons onto the planet. Falcon began to retract all the instrument booms that were extended out from the capsule. There were no other precautions he could take. It would be four hours before the atmospheric shock wave reached him—but the radio blast, traveling at the speed of light, would be here in a tenth of a second, once the discharge had been triggered.

The radio monitor, scanning back and forth across the spectrum, still showed nothing unusual, just the normal mush of background static. Then Falcon noticed that the noise level was slowly creeping upward. The explosion was gathering its strength.

At such a distance he had never expected to *see* anything. But suddenly a flicker as of far-off heat lightning danced along the eastern horizon. Simultaneously, half the circuit breakers jumped out of the main switchboard, the lights failed, and all communications channels went dead.

He tried to move, but was completely unable to do so. The paralysis that gripped him was not merely psychological; he seemed to have lost all control of his limbs and could feel a painful tingling sensation over his entire body. It was impossible that the electric field could have penetrated this shielded cabin. Yet there was a flickering glow over the instrument board, and he could hear the unmistakable crackle of a brush discharge.

With a series of sharp bangs, the emergency systems went into operation, and the overloads reset themselves. The lights flickered on again. And Falcon's paralysis disappeared as swiftly as it had come.

After glancing at the board to make sure that all circuits were back to normal, he moved quickly to the viewing ports.

There was no need to switch on the inspection lamps—the cables supporting the capsule seemed to be on fire. Lines of light glowing an electric blue against the darkness stretched upward from the main lift ring to the equator of the giant balloon; and rolling slowly along several of them were dazzling balls of fire.

The sight was so strange and so beautiful that it was hard to read any menace in it. Few people, Falcon knew, had ever seen ball lightning from such close quarters—and certainly none had survived if they were riding a hydrogen-filled balloon back in the atmosphere of Earth. He remembered the flaming death of the *Hindenburg,* destroyed by a stray spark when she docked at Lakehurst in 1937; as it had done so often in the past, the horrifying old newsreel film flashed through his mind. But at least that could not happen here, though there was more hydrogen above his head than had ever filled the last of the Zeppelins. It would be a few billion years yet, before anyone could light a fire in the atmosphere of Jupiter.

With a sound like briskly frying bacon, the speech circuit came back to life.

"Hello, *Kon-Tiki*—are you receiving? Are you receiving?"

The words were chopped and badly distorted, but intelligible. Falcon's spirits lifted; he had resumed contact with the world of men.

"I receive you," he said. "Quite an electrical display, but no damage—so far."

"Thanks—thought we'd lost you. Please check telemetry channels three, seven, twenty-six. Also gain on camera two. And we don't quite believe the readings on the external ionization probes. . . ."

Reluctantly Falcon tore his gaze away from the fascinating pyrotechnic display around *Kon-Tiki,* though from time to time he kept glancing out of the windows. The ball lightning disappeared first, the fiery globes slowly expanding until they reached a critical size, at which they vanished in a gentle explosion. But even an hour later, there were still faint glows around all the exposed metal on the outside of the capsule; and the radio circuits remained noisy until well after midnight.

The remaining hours of darkness were completely uneventful—until just before dawn. Because it came from the east, Falcon assumed that he was seeing the first faint hint of sunrise. Then he realized that it was twenty minutes too early for this—and the glow that had appeared along the horizon was moving toward him even as he watched. It swiftly detached itself from the arch of stars that marked the invisible edge of the planet, and he saw that it was a relatively narrow band, quite sharply defined. The beam of an enormous searchlight appeared to be swinging beneath the clouds.

Perhaps sixty miles behind the first racing bar of light came another, parallel to it and moving at the same speed. And beyond that another, and another—until all the sky flickered with alternating sheets of light and darkness.

By this time, Falcon thought, he had been inured to wonders, and it seemed impossible that this display of pure, soundless luminosity could present the slightest danger. But it was so astonishing, and so inexplicable, that he felt cold, naked fear gnawing at his self-control. No man could look upon such a sight without feeling like a helpless pygmy in the presence of forces beyond his comprehension. Was it possible that, after all, Jupiter carried not only life but also intelligence? And, perhaps, an intelligence that only now was beginning to react to his alien presence?

"Yes, we see it," said Mission Control, in a voice that echoed his own awe. "We've no idea what it is. Stand by, we're calling Ganymede."

The display was slowly fading; the bands racing in from the far horizon were much fainter, as if the energies that powered them were becoming exhausted. In five minutes it was all over; the last faint pulse of light flickered along the western sky and then was gone. Its passing left Falcon with an overwhelming sense of relief. The sight was so hypnotic, and so disturbing, that it was not good for any man's peace of mind to contemplate it too long.

He was more shaken than he cared to admit. The electrical storm was something that he could understand; but *this* was totally incomprehensible.

Mission Control was still silent. He knew that the information banks up on Ganymede were now being searched as men and computers turned their minds to the problem. If no answer could be found there, it would be necessary to call Earth; that would mean a delay of almost an hour. The possibility that even Earth might be unable to help was one that Falcon did not care to contemplate.

He had never before been so glad to hear the voice of Mission Control as when Dr. Brenner finally came on the circuit. The biologist sounded relieved, yet subdued—like a man who has just come through some great intellectual crisis.

"Hello, *Kon-Tiki*. We've solved your problem, but we can still hardly believe it.

"What you've been seeing is bioluminescence, very similar to that produced by microorganisms in the tropical seas of Earth. Here they're in the atmosphere, not the ocean, but the principle is the same."

"But the pattern," protested Falcon, "was so regular—so *artificial*. And it was hundreds of miles across!"

"It was even larger than you imagine; you observed only a small part of it. The whole pattern was over three thousand miles wide and looked like a revolving wheel. You merely saw the spokes, sweeping past you at about six-tenths of a mile a second. . . ."

"A *second!*" Falcon could not help interjecting. "No animals could move that fast!"

"Of course not. Let me explain. What you saw was triggered by the shock wave from Source Beta, moving at the speed of sound."

"But what about the pattern?" Falcon insisted.

"That's the surprising part. It's a very rare phenomenon, but identical wheels of light—except that they're a thousand times smaller—have been observed in the Persian Gulf and the Indian Ocean. Listen to this: British India Company's *Patna,* Persian Gulf, May 1880, 11:30 P.M.—'an enormous luminous wheel, whirling round, the spokes of which appeared to brush the ship along. The spokes were 200 or 300 yards long . . . each wheel contained about sixteen spokes. . . .' And here's one from the Gulf of Omar, dated May 23, 1906: 'The intensely bright luminescence approached us rapidly, shooting sharply defined light rays to the west in rapid succession, like the beam from the searchlight of a warship. . . . To the left of us, a gigantic fiery wheel formed itself, with spokes that reached as far as one could see. The whole wheel whirled around for two or three minutes. . . .' The archive computer on Ganymede dug up about five hundred cases. It would have printed out the lot if we hadn't stopped it in time."

"I'm convinced—but still baffled."

"I don't blame you. The full explanation wasn't worked out until late in the twentieth century. It seems that these luminous wheels are the results of submarine earthquakes, and always occur in shallow waters where the shock waves can be reflected and cause standing wave patterns. Sometimes bars, sometimes rotating wheels—the 'Wheels of Poseidon,' they've been called. The theory was finally proved by making underwater explosions and photographing the results from a satellite. No wonder sailors used to be superstitious. Who would have believed a thing like *this?*"

So that was it, Falcon told himself. When Source Beta

blew its top, it must have sent shock waves in all directions—through the compressed gas of the lower atmosphere, through the solid body of Jupiter itself. Meeting and crisscrossing, those waves must have canceled here, reinforced there; the whole planet must have rung like a bell.

Yet the explanation did not destroy the sense of wonder and awe; he would never be able to forget those flickering bands of light, racing through the unattainable depths of the Jovian atmosphere. He felt that he was not merely on a strange planet, but in some magical realm between myth and reality.

This was a world where absolutely *anything* could happen, and no man could possibly guess what the future would bring.

And he still had a whole day to go.

6. MEDUSA

When the true dawn finally arrived, it brought a sudden change of weather. *Kon-Tiki* was moving through a blizzard; waxen snowflakes were falling so thickly that visibility was reduced to zero. Falcon began to worry about the weight that might be accumulating on the envelope. Then he noticed that any flakes settling outside the windows quickly disappeared; *Kon-Tiki*'s continual outpouring of heat was evaporating them as swiftly as they arrived.

If he had been ballooning on Earth, he would also have worried about the possibility of collision. At least that was no danger here; any Jovian mountains were several hundred miles below him. And as for the floating islands of foam, hitting them would probably be like plowing into slightly hardened soap bubbles.

Nevertheless, he switched on the horizontal radar, which until now had been completely useless; only the vertical beam, giving his distance from the invisible surface, had thus far been of any value. Then he had another surprise.

Scattered across a huge sector of the sky ahead were dozens of large and brilliant echoes. They were completely isolated from one another and apparently hung unsupported in space. Falcon remembered a phrase the earliest aviators had used to describe one of the hazards of their profession: "clouds stuffed with rocks." That was a perfect description of what seemed to lie in the track of *Kon-Tiki*.

It was a disconcerting sight; then Falcon again reminded himself that nothing *really* solid could possibly hover in this atmosphere. Perhaps it was some strange meteorological phenomenon. In any case, the nearest echo was about a hundred and twenty-five miles.

He reported to Mission Control, which could provide no explanation. But it gave the welcome news that he would be clear of the blizzard in another thirty minutes.

It did not warn him, however, of the violent cross wind that abruptly grabbed *Kon-Tiki* and swept it almost at right angles to its previous track. Falcon needed all his skill and the maximum use of what little control he had over his ungainly vehicle to prevent it from being capsized. Within minutes he was racing northward at over three hundred miles an hour. Then, as suddenly as it had started, the turbulence ceased; he was still moving at high speed, but in smooth air. He wondered if he had been caught in the Jovian equivalent of a jet stream.

The snow storm dissolved; and he saw what Jupiter had been preparing for him.

Kon-Tiki had entered the funnel of a gigantic whirlpool, some six hundred miles across. The balloon was being swept along a curving wall of cloud. Overhead, the sun was shining in a clear sky; but far beneath, this great hole in the atmosphere drilled down to unknown depths until it reached a misty floor where lightning flickered almost continuously.

Though the vessel was being dragged downward so slowly that it was in no immediate danger, Falcon increased the flow of heat into the envelope until *Kon-Tiki* hovered at a constant altitude. Not until then did he abandon the fantastic spectacle outside and consider again the problem of the radar.

The nearest echo was now only about twenty-five miles away. All of them, he quickly realized, were distributed along the wall of the vortex, and were moving with it, apparently caught in the whirlpool like *Kon-Tiki* itself. He aimed the telescope along the radar bearing and found himself looking at a curious mottled cloud that almost filled the field of view.

It was not easy to see, being only a little darker than the whirling wall of mist that formed its background. Not until he had been staring for several minutes did Falcon realize that he had met it once before.

The first time it had been crawling across the drifting mountains of foam, and he had mistaken it for a giant, many-trunked tree. Now at last he could appreciate its real size and complexity and could give it a better name to fix its image in his mind. It did not resemble a tree at all, but a jellyfish—a medusa, such as might be met trailing its tentacles as it drifted along the warm eddies of the Gulf Stream.

This medusa was more than a mile across and its scores of dangling tentacles were hundreds of feet long. They swayed slowly back and forth in perfect unison, taking more than a minute for each complete undulation—almost as if the creature was clumsily rowing itself through the sky.

The other echoes were more distant medusae. Falcon focused the telescope on half a dozen and could see no variations in shape or size. They all seemed to be of the same species, and he wondered just why they were drifting lazily around in this six-hundred-mile orbit. Perhaps they were feeding upon the aerial plankton sucked in by the whirlpool, as *Kon-Tiki* itself had been.

"Do you realize, Howard," said Dr. Brenner, when he had recovered from his initial astonishment, "that this thing is about a hundred thousand times as large as the biggest whale? And even if it's only a gasbag, it must still weigh a million tons! I can't even guess at its metabolism. It must generate megawatts of heat to maintain its buoyancy."

"But if it's just a gasbag, why is it such a damn good radar reflector?"

"I haven't the faintest idea. Can you get any closer?"

Brenner's question was not an idle one. If he changed altitude to take advantage of the differing wind velocities,

Falcon could approach the medusa as closely as he wished. At the moment, however, he preferred his present twenty-five miles and said so, firmly.

"I see what you mean," Brenner answered, a little reluctantly. "Let's stay where we are for the present." That "we" gave Falcon a certain wry amusement; an extra sixty thousand miles made a considerable difference in one's point of view.

For the next two hours *Kon-Tiki* drifted uneventfully in the gyre of the great whirlpool, while Falcon experimented with filters and camera contrast, trying to get a clear view of the medusa. He began to wonder if its elusive coloration was some kind of camouflage; perhaps, like many animals of Earth, it was trying to lose itself against its background. That was a trick used by both hunters and hunted.

In which category was the medusa? That was a question he could hardly expect to have answered in the short time that was left to him. Yet just before noon, without the slightest warning, the answer came. . . .

Like a squadron of antique jet fighters, five mantas came sweeping through the wall of mist that formed the funnel of the vortex. They were flying in a V formation directly toward the pallid gray cloud of the medusa; and there was no doubt, in Falcon's mind, that they were on the attack. He had been quite wrong to assume that they were harmless vegetarians.

Yet everything happened at such a leisurely pace that it was like watching a slow-motion film. The mantas undulated along at perhaps thirty miles an hour; it seemed ages before they reached the medusa, which continued to paddle imperturbably along at an even slower speed. Huge though they were, the mantas looked tiny beside the monster they were approaching. When they flapped down on its back, they appeared about as large as birds landing on a whale.

Could the medusa defend itself, Falcon wondered. He did not see how the attacking mantas could be in danger as long as they avoided those huge clumsy tentacles. And perhaps their host was not even aware of them; they could be insignificant parasites, tolerated as are fleas upon a dog.

But now it was obvious that the medusa was in distress.

With agonizing slowness, it began to tip over like a capsizing ship. After ten minutes it had tilted forty-five degrees; it was also rapidly losing altitude. It was impossible not to feel a sense of pity for the beleaguered monster, and to Falcon the sight brought bitter memories. In a grotesque way, the fall of the medusa was almost a parody of the dying *Queen*'s last moments.

Yet he knew that his sympathies were on the wrong side. High intelligence could develop only among predators—not among the drifting browsers of either sea or air. The mantas were far closer to him than was this monstrous bag of gas. And anyway, who could *really* sympathize with a creature a hundred thousand times larger than a whale?

Then he noticed that the medusa's tactics seemed to be having some effect. The mantas had been disturbed by its slow roll and were flapping heavily away from its back—like gorged vultures interrupted at mealtime. But they did not move very far, continuing to hover a few yards from the still-capsizing monster.

There was a sudden, blinding flash of light synchronized with a crash of static over the radio. One of the mantas, slowly twisting end over end, was plummeting straight downward. As it fell, a plume of black smoke trailed behind it. The resemblance to an aircraft going down in flames was quite uncanny.

In unison, the remaining mantas dived steeply away from the medusa, gaining speed by losing altitude. They had, within minutes, vanished back into the wall of cloud from which they had emerged. And the medusa, no longer falling, began to roll back toward the horizontal. Soon it was sailing along once more on an even keel, as if nothing had happened.

"Beautiful!" said Dr. Brenner, after a moment of stunned silence. "It's developed electric defenses, like some of our eels and rays. But that must have been about a million volts! Can you see any organs that might produce the discharge? Anything looking like electrodes?"

"No," Falcon answered, after switching to the highest

power of the telescope. "But here's something odd. Do you see this pattern? Check back on the earlier images. I'm sure it wasn't there before."

A broad, mottled band had appeared along the side of the medusa. It formed a startlingly regular checkerboard, each square of which was itself speckled in a complex subpattern of short horizontal lines. They were spaced at equal distances in a geometrically perfect array of rows and columns.

"You're right," said Dr. Brenner, with something very much like awe in his voice. "That's just appeared. And I'm afraid to tell you what I think it is."

"Well, I have no reputation to lose—at least as a biologist. Shall I give my guess?"

"Go ahead."

"That's a large meter-band radio array. The sort of thing they used back at the beginning of the twentieth century."

"I was afraid you'd say that. Now we know why it gave such a massive echo."

"But why has it just appeared?"

"Probably an aftereffect of the discharge."

"I've just had another thought," said Falcon, rather slowly. "Do you suppose it's *listening* to us?"

"On this frequency? I doubt it. Those are meter—no, *decameter* antennas—judging by their size. Hmm . . . that's an idea!"

Dr. Brenner fell silent, obviously contemplating some new line of thought. Presently he continued: "I bet they're tuned to the radio outbursts! That's something nature never got around to doing on Earth. . . . We have animals with sonar and even electric senses, but nothing ever developed a radio sense. Why bother where there was so much light?

"But it's different here. Jupiter is *drenched* with radio energy. It's worth while using it—maybe even tapping it. That thing could be a floating power plant!"

A new voice cut into the conversation.

"Mission Commander here. This is all very interesting, but there's a much more important matter to settle. *Is it intelli-*

gent? If so, we've got to consider the First Contact directives."

"Until I came here," said Dr. Brenner, somewhat ruefully, "I would have sworn that anything that could make a short-wave antenna system *must* be intelligent. Now, I'm not sure. This could have evolved naturally. I suppose it's no more fantastic than the human eye."

"Then we have to play safe and assume intelligence. For the present, therefore, this expedition comes under all the clauses of the Prime directive."

There was a long silence while everyone on the radio circuit absorbed the implications of this. For the first time in the history of space flight, the rules that had been established through more than a century of argument might have to be applied. Man had—it was hoped—profited from his mistakes on Earth. Not only moral considerations, but also his own self-interest demanded that he should not repeat them among the planets. It could be disastrous to treat a superior intelligence as the American settlers had treated the Indians, or as almost everyone had treated the Africans. . . .

The first rule was: keep your distance. Make no attempt to approach, or even to communicate, until "they" have had plenty of time to study you. Exactly what was meant by "plenty of time," no one had ever been able to decide. It was left to the discretion of the man on the spot.

A responsibility of which he had never dreamed had descended upon Howard Falcon. In the few hours that remained to him on Jupiter, he might become the first ambassador of the human race.

And *that* was an irony so delicious that he almost wished the surgeons had restored to him the power of laughter.

7. PRIME DIRECTIVE

It was growing darker, but Falcon scarcely noticed as he strained his eyes toward that living cloud in the field of the telescope. The wind that was steadily sweeping *Kon-Tiki* around the funnel of the great whirlpool had now brought him within twelve miles of the creature. If he got much closer than six, he would take evasive action. Though he felt certain that the medusa's electric weapons were short ranged, he did not wish to put the matter to the test. That would be a problem for future explorers, and he wished them luck.

Now it was quite dark in the capsule. That was strange, because sunset was still hours away. Automatically, he glanced at the horizontally scanning radar, as he had done every few minutes. Apart from the medusa he was studying, there was no other object within about sixty miles of him.

Suddenly, with startling power, he heard the sound that had come booming out of the Jovian night—the throbbing beat that grew more and more rapid, then stopped in mid-crescendo. The whole capsule vibrated with it like a pea in a kettledrum.

Falcon realized two things almost simultaneously during the sudden, aching silence. *This* time the sound was not coming from thousands of miles away, over a radio circuit. It was in the very atmosphere around him.

The second thought was even more disturbing. He had quite forgotten—it was inexcusable, but there had been other apparently more important things on his mind—that most of the sky above him was completely blanked out by *Kon-Tiki*'s gasbag. Being lightly silvered to conserve its heat, the great balloon was an effective shield both to radar and to vision.

He had known this, of course; it had been a minor defect of the design, tolerated because it did not appear important. It seemed very important to Howard Falcon now—as he saw that fence of gigantic tentacles, thicker than the trunks of any tree, descending all around the capsule.

He heard Brenner yelling: "Remember the Prime directive! Don't alarm it!" Before he could make an appropriate answer that overwhelming drumbeat started again and drowned all other sounds.

The sign of a really skilled test pilot is how he reacts not to foreseeable emergencies, but to ones that nobody could have anticipated. Falcon did not hesitate for more than a second to analyze the situation. In a lightning-swift movement, he pulled the rip cord.

That word was an archaic survival from the days of the first hydrogen balloons; on *Kon-Tiki,* the rip cord did not tear open the gasbag, but merely operated a set of louvers around the upper curve of the envelope. At once the hot gas started to rush out; *Kon-Tiki,* deprived of her lift, began to fall swiftly in this gravity field two and a half times as strong as Earth's.

Falcon had a momentary glimpse of great tentacles whipping upward and away. He had just time to note that they were studded with large bladders or sacs, presumably to give them buoyancy, and that they ended in multitudes of thin feelers like the roots of a plant. He half expected a bolt of lightning—but nothing happened.

His precipitous rate of descent was slackening as the atmosphere thickened and the deflated envelope acted as a parachute. When *Kon-Tiki* had dropped about two miles, he felt that it was safe to close the louvers again. By the time he had restored buoyancy and was in equilibrium once more, he had lost another mile of altitude and was getting dangerously near his safety limit.

He peered anxiously through the overhead windows, though he did not expect to see anything except the obscuring bulk of the balloon. But he had sideslipped during his descent, and part of the medusa was just visible a couple of miles above him. It was much closer than he expected—and it was still coming down, faster than he would have believed possible.

Mission Control was calling anxiously. He shouted: "I'm O.K.—but it's still coming after me. I can't go any deeper."

That was not quite true. He could go a lot deeper—about one hundred and eighty miles. But it would be a one-way trip, and most of the journey would be of little interest to him.

Then, to his great relief, he saw that the medusa was leveling off, not quite a mile above him. Perhaps it had decided to approach this strange intruder with caution; or perhaps it, too, found this deeper layer uncomfortably hot. The temperature was over fifty degrees centigrade, and Falcon wondered how much longer his life-support system could handle matters.

Dr. Brenner was back on the circuit, still worrying about the Prime directive.

"Remember—it may only be inquisitive!" he cried, without much conviction. "Try not to frighten it!"

Falcon was getting rather tired of this advice and recalled a TV discussion he had once seen between a space lawyer and an astronaut. After the full implications of the Prime directive had been carefully spelled out, the incredulous spacer had exclaimed: "Then if there was no alternative, I must sit still and let myself be eaten?" The lawyer had not even cracked a smile when he answered: "That's an *excellent* summing up."

It had seemed funny at the time; it was not at all amusing now.

And then Falcon saw something that made him even more unhappy. The medusa was still hovering about a mile above him—but one of its tentacles was becoming incredibly elongated, and was stretching down toward *Kon-Tiki,* thinning out at the same time. As a boy he had once seen the funnel of a tornado descending from a storm cloud over the Kansas plains. The thing coming toward him now evoked vivid memories of that black, twisting snake in the sky.

"I'm rapidly running out of options," he reported to Mission Control. "I now have only a choice between frightening it—and giving it a bad stomach-ache. I don't think it will find *Kon-Tiki* very digestible, if that's what it has in mind."

He waited for comments from Brenner, but the biologist remained silent.

"Very well. It's twenty-seven minutes ahead of time, but I'm starting the ignition sequencer. I hope I'll have enough reserve to correct my orbit later."

He could no longer see the medusa; once more it was directly overhead. But he knew that the descending tentacle must now be very close to the balloon. It would take almost five minutes to bring the reactor up to full thrust. . . .

The fusor was primed. The orbit computer had not rejected the situation as wholly impossible. The air scoops were open, ready to gulp in tons of the surrounding hydrohelium on demand. Even under optimum conditions, this would have been the moment of truth—for there had been no way of testing how a nuclear ramjet would *really* work in the strange atmosphere of Jupiter.

Very gently something rocked *Kon-Tiki.* Falcon tried to ignore it.

Ignition had been planned at six miles higher, in an atmosphere of less than a quarter of the density and thirty degrees cooler. Too bad.

What was the shallowest dive he could get away with, for the air scoops to work? When the ram ignited, he'd be heading toward Jupiter with two and a half g's to help him get there. Could he possibly pull out in time?

A large, heavy hand patted the balloon. The whole vessel bobbed up and down, like one of the Yo-yo's that had just become the craze on Earth.

Of course, Brenner *might* be perfectly right. Perhaps it was just trying to be friendly. Maybe he should try to talk to it over the radio. Which should it be: "Pretty pussy"? "Down, Fido"? Or "Take me to your leader"?

The tritium-deuterium ratio was correct. He was ready to light the candle, with a hundred-million-degree match.

The thin tip of the tentacle came slithering around the edge of the balloon some sixty yards away. It was about the size of an elephant's trunk, and by the delicate way it was moving appeared to be almost as sensitive. There were little palps at its end, like questing mouths. He was sure that Dr. Brenner would be fascinated.

This seemed about as good a time as any. He gave a swift scan of the entire control board, started the final four-second ignition count, broke the safety seal, and pressed the JETTISON switch.

There was a sharp explosion and an instant loss of weight. *Kon-Tiki* was falling freely, nose down. Overhead, the discarded balloon was racing upward, dragging the inquisitive tentacle with it. Falcon had no time to see if the gasbag actually hit the medusa, because at that moment the ramjet fired and he had other matters to think about.

A roaring column of hot hydrohelium was pouring out of the reactor nozzles, swiftly building up thrust—but *toward* Jupiter, not away from it. He could not pull out yet, for vector control was too sluggish. Unless he could gain complete control and achieve horizontal flight within the next five seconds, the vehicle would dive too deeply into the atmosphere and would be destroyed.

With agonizing slowness—those five seconds seemed like fifty—he managed to flatten out, then pull the nose upward. He glanced back only once and caught a final glimpse of the medusa, many miles away. *Kon-Tiki*'s discarded gasbag had apparently escaped from its grasp, for he could see no sign of it.

Now he was master once more—no longer drifting helplessly on the winds of Jupiter, but riding his own column of atomic fire back to the stars. He was confident that the ramjet would steadily give him velocity and altitude until he had reached near-orbital speed at the fringes of the atmosphere. Then, with a brief burst of pure rocket power, he would regain the freedom of space.

Halfway to orbit, he looked south and saw the tremendous enigma of the Great Red Spot—that floating island twice the size of Earth—coming up over the horizon. He stared into its mysterious beauty until the computer warned him that conversion to rocket thrust was only sixty seconds ahead. He tore his gaze reluctantly away.

"Some other time," he murmured.

"What's that?" said Mission Control. "What did you say?"

"It doesn't matter," he replied.

8. BETWEEN TWO WORLDS

"You're a hero now, Howard," said Webster, "not just a celebrity. You've given them something to think about—injected some excitement into their lives. Not one in a million will actually travel to the Outer Giants, but the whole human race will go in imagination. And that's what counts."

"I'm glad to have made your job a little easier."

Webster was too old a friend to take offense at the note of irony. Yet it surprised him. And this was not the first change in Howard that he had noticed since the return from Jupiter.

The Administrator pointed to the famous sign on his desk, borrowed from an impresario of an earlier age: ASTONISH ME!

"I'm not ashamed of my job. New knowledge, new resources—they're all very well. But men also need novelty and excitement. Space travel has become routine; you've made it a great adventure once more. It will be a long, long time before we get Jupiter pigeonholed. And maybe longer still before we understand those medusae. I still think that one *knew* where your blind spot was. Anyway, have you decided on your next move? Saturn, Uranus, Neptune—you name it."

"I don't know. I've thought about Saturn, but I'm not really needed there. It's only one gravity, not two and a half like Jupiter. So men can handle it."

Men, thought Webster. He said "men." He's never done that before. And when did I last hear him use the word "we"? He's changing, slipping away from us. . . .

"Well," he said aloud, rising from his chair to conceal his slight uneasiness, "let's get the conference started. The cameras are all set up and everyone's waiting. You'll meet a lot of old friends."

He stressed the last word, but Howard showed no response. The leathery mask of his face was becoming more and more difficult to read. Instead, he rolled back from the Administrator's desk, unlocked his undercarriage so that it no longer formed a chair, and rose on his hydraulics to his full seven feet of height. It had been good psychology on the part of the surgeons to give him that extra twelve inches, to compensate somewhat for all that he had lost when the *Queen* had crashed.

Falcon waited until Webster had opened the door, then pivoted neatly on his balloon tires and headed for it at a smooth and silent twenty miles an hour. The display of speed and precision was not flaunted arrogantly; rather, it had become quite unconscious.

Howard Falcon, who had once been a man and could still pass for one over a voice circuit, felt a calm sense of achievement—and, for the first time in years, something like peace of mind. Since his return from Jupiter, the nightmares had ceased. He had found his role at last.

He now knew why he had dreamed about that superchimp aboard the doomed *Queen Elizabeth*. Neither man nor beast, it was between two worlds; and so was he.

He alone could travel unprotected on the lunar surface. The life-support system inside the metal cylinder that had replaced his fragile body functioned equally well in space or under water. Gravity fields ten times that of Earth were an inconvenience, but nothing more. And no gravity was best of all. . . .

The human race was becoming more remote, the ties of kinship more tenuous. Perhaps these air-breathing, radiation-sensitive bundles of unstable carbon compounds had no right beyond the atmosphere; they should stick to their natural homes—Earth, Moon, Mars.

Some day the real masters of space would be machines, not men—and he was neither. Already conscious of his destiny, he took a somber pride in his unique loneliness—the first immortal midway between two orders of creation.

He would, after all, be an ambassador; between the old and the new—between the creatures of carbon and the creatures of metal who must one day supersede them.

Both would have need of him in the troubled centuries that lay ahead.

February 1971

Fairyland

PAUL J. McAULEY

In twenty-first-century Europe, endlessly ravaged by the changes of war and technology, gene hacker and psychoactive virus designer Alex Sharkey is a bare step ahead of the police and the Triads. But when he helps a scarily super-smart little girl called Milena to turn a genetically engineered Doll into the first of a new, autonomous species, the Fairies, he doesn't realize he's giving history a dangerous shove.

Milena has her own reasons. Some of the Folk, as fey and malign as any in legend, have other ideas about their destiny . . .

A giddyingly baroque journey through the crumbling counter-cultures, obsolete magic kingdoms and war-torn realities of post-nanotech Europe.

'McAuley is part of a spearhead of writers who for pure imagination, hipness, vision and fun have made Britain the Memphis Sun Records of SF'
Mail on Sunday

£5.99 0 575 60031 4

Timescape

GREGORY BENFORD

1998: the world is a growing nightmare of desperation, uncontrollable pollution and terrifying social unrest. In Cambridge two scientists experimenting with subatomic particles realize that they could send a message – a warning to the past, to the previous generation.

A warning that says: *Stop. Before it's too late. Before you condemn your own children to death.*

1962: a young Californian scientist finds his experiments are being spoiled by mysterious interference. As his suspicions edge nearer to the truth, it becomes a race against time – for in his future the world is collapsing and will only survive if he can decipher the shattering, incredible messages in time . . .

'Fascinating...grippingly readable' *Daily Telegraph*

£5.99 0 575 60050 5

Mortal Remains

CHRISTOPHER EVANS

The solar system is ours. Biotechnology has provided the Settled Worlds with a riot of habitable environments; sentient craft ply the routes between the planets; the souls of the dead live on in the Noosphere, a psychic Net where they can be contacted by the living.

Paradise? Not quite – and when a strange womb is recovered from a living spaceship crashed on Mars it swiftly becomes the focus of intrigue and murder as the Settled Worlds begin to disintegrate under the strain of vicious interplanetary war between two rival factions.

£8.99 0 575 06155 3

Other Vista SF and Fantasy titles include

The Difference Engine William Gibson & Bruce Sterling 0 575 60029 2

A Land Fit for Heroes vol 3: The Dragon Wakes Phillip Mann 0 575 60012 8

Terry Pratchett's Discworld Quizbook David Langford 0 575 60000 4

Eric Terry Pratchett 0 575 60001 2

Lethe Tricia Sullivan 0 575 60039 X

Mortal Remains Christopher Evans 0 575 60043 8

Golden Witchbreed Mary Gentle 0 575 60033 0

The Knights of the Black Earth Margaret Weis & Don Perrin 0 575 60037 3

Fairyland Paul J. McAuley 0 575 60031 4

Sailing Bright Eternity Gregory Benford 0 575 60047 0

Timescape Gregory Benford 0 575 60050 0

Reach for Tomorrow Arthur C. Clarke 0 575 60046 2

The Wind from the Sun Arthur C. Clarke 0 575 60052 7

Hawkwood's Voyage Paul Kearney 0 575 60034 9

Chaga Ian McDonald 0 575 60022 5